DONNELL: COWBOY SCRUTINY

THE KAVANAGH BROTHERS BOOK 5

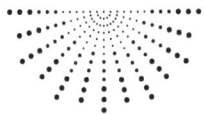

KATHLEEN BALL

Copyright © 2020 by Kathleen Ball

All rights reserved.

No part of this book may be reproduced in any form or by any electronic or mechanical means, including information storage and retrieval systems, without written permission from the author, except for the use of brief quotations in a book review.

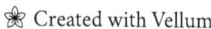 Created with Vellum

CHAPTER ONE

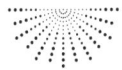

The trunk sat directly in Donnell Kavanagh's path on the planked walkway. He frowned as he side-stepped it to avoid running into it. Muttering under his breath, he shook his head. Why didn't people just put things where they belonged? Against the front of the general store would have worked. Anywhere but right where people walked.

He pushed the door open, jingling the bells above it. The housekeeper on the Kavanagh ranch had sent him to town with a list of items. He had nine brothers, but she had asked him. He had plenty of work, enough to keep him busy for months. No one said no to Dolly, though. He wasn't even sure what made her choose him. Maybe she figured the importance of his work didn't exist.

"Good to see you, John," he greeted the store owner, who nodded at him when he walked inside.

A woman stood at the counter, which meant he'd have to wait his turn, so he wandered around the store, checking out the shelves. After he looked around, he walked closer to the back of the store hoping to find out what was taking John so long with the other customer.

He tried to get a look at the woman, but her calico bonnet hid many of her features. Wisps of her blond hair had escaped but that was all he could make out. He observed the collection of dust on her clothes and surmised she'd taken the coach.

"I'm sorry, really I am, but no one by the name Joe Kingsley lives in these here parts," John O'Rourke said, the impatience in his voice was very clear.

Her shoulders slumped. "Thank you anyway. I should have known this would happen." She turned and walked out of the store without so much as a glance at Donnell.

"Poor woman," John said, shaking his head. "She's a mail-order bride, but there isn't a groom. Well, what brings you here, Donnell? Did Dolly send you with a list?"

Donnell handed the piece of paper to the shopkeeper.

After glancing at the items listed, John smiled. "I'll have this order ready for you in about ten minutes."

"Thanks, I'll be back." Donnell strode back outside to the wooden plank walk. The woman from the store was sitting on her trunk and when she gazed up at him, she had all kinds of hurt in her eyes.

"Anything I can do to help?" As soon as the words were out of his mouth, he wanted them back. What was he doing? He always became entangled when he helped.

"No but thank you for asking." A heavy sigh slipped out. "Is there a boarding house near here? I saw a hotel, but I can't afford that. I thought maybe I could do some work in exchange for a room."

"It's all full up!" John called from inside.

Her forehead wrinkled. "He heard us from all the way in there?"

Before Donnell could answer, John yelled, "Yes!"

Donnell's lips twitched. John knew all the latest happenings around town. He offered his arm to the woman. "Let's walk and let John have some peace."

She hesitated, and he thought for sure she'd say no, but she finally stood and put her arm on his. Her touch warmed him.

"I'm Donnell Kavanagh, and you are?"

"I'm Clarissa Plunkett. We must make this a brief walk; I need to find a place to spend the night."

"Tell me what happened," he suggested.

"I had been corresponding with Mr. Kingsley for three months. I know that's not very long, seeing it takes a while to get a letter delivered, but we both believed we suited. He sent me a ticket and a proposal. Well, no one met me when I got off the stagecoach, I got a funny feeling. Honestly, I don't know what to make of my situation. He seemed sincere, and I'm not the most trusting woman."

"It's perplexing, all right. I've never heard of a Joe Kingsley either. Are you sure you're in the right town? Maybe you got on the wrong stagecoach. Or got off at the wrong stop?"

"Thank you for the walk, Mr. Kavanagh. I think I'll stop in at the hotel after all." She slipped her hand from his arm and went into the hotel.

Donnell waited a few minutes, but she didn't come back out. He shrugged; she'd be just fine. He hurried back to the store and was glad to see that John had everything ready to be loaded into the wagon.

"So, did you get any information on that pretty gal?"

Donnell shook his head. "She looks too young to be on her own. I'm sure she'll get it figured out." As soon as everything was in the wagon, Donnell went back into the store. "If she's in trouble have someone ride out to get me." He headed for home. He tried to think about all the work he had to do, but Clarissa's troubled face distracted him.

CLARISSA PULLED her wrap around her. The sun would set in about an hour. She'd waited until the pleasant man, Donnell, had left town to come out of the hotel lobby. He was sympathetic, but he didn't have any answers. All the businesses were closing up, all except for the saloon. They probably had a cheap room, but she'd counted on making a fresh start. She wanted to be known as a respectable woman. A woman Joe Kingsley would be proud of.

She hurried across the street and went through the saloon's swinging doors. It was like walking into a cloud of smoke.

"If you ain't drinkin' you ain't stayin'!" the bartender shouted at her.

Heat scorched her face as every man in the place turned to stare at her. If she wanted to sleep inside, she'd have to go to the bar. Pretending she wasn't being watched, that was just what she did. The bartender wore such an amused expression, she felt all kinds of humiliated.

"Would you like whiskey or whiskey?" He leaned his arm onto the bar as he continued to stare at her.

"How much is a whiskey?" she asked, trying to sound confident.

"If you need to ask, you can't afford one. Whatcha doing here? This is no place for you."

"I need a room for the night. I got off at the wrong stop." She jutted her jaw and met his gaze. "I don't want a job here, just a room."

"Honey, if you can't afford a whiskey you can't afford a

room. There's a boarding house on the other side of the street."

"It's filled." She nodded in his direction. "Thank you anyway. It won't be the first time I've slept outside." She turned and walked to the doors.

"Wait, you can stay free for one night. Is that your trunk that's been sitting in front of the general store all day?"

She nodded.

"I'll have one of the fellas get it for you." He handed her a key. "Room five and make sure you keep the door locked. I can't help it if the men knock, just don't open the door."

Shocked, she tried to cover her shaking as she took the key. "Thank you. It's the kindest thing anyone has done for me in a very long time."

He gave her a sad smile and pointed to the stairs. She walked as primly and properly as she could while men whistled and made crude remarks. Slowly, she climbed the steps. This was not the beginning of her fresh start.

IF DONNELL HAD to hear about that poor girl one more time he was going to eat in the bunkhouse. How did news travel so fast? It was all too suspicious as far as he was concerned. She was just a woman.

It wasn't his problem. Really it was not his problem. Nope, not his. He sighed. If he hoped for any peace, he'd best see Miss. Plunkett. He'd be firm. An offer of money would be the only thing to do no matter what Dolly wanted. He'd get Miss. Plunkett onto a stagecoach going somewhere else. Perhaps he should have just taken her home to the ranch yesterday. He always thought of the nice thing to do later, never in the moment.

He went to the barn and his other brothers snickered as

he saddled Rascal, his roan gelding. He didn't glance at his brothers or utter a word. The leather saddle creaked as he jumped on. He lowered the brim of his tan hat and urged his horse into a leisurely walk as he rode toward town.

It wasn't a lengthy ride and the day was pleasant enough. He stopped Rascal in front of the hotel, slid off and then tied the horse at the hitching post. He nodded in greeting to a few folks out walking and went into the hotel.

The owner of the hotel, Glen Pickford, was a good man and an excellent friend. Donnell shook his hand. "Has Miss. Plunkett come down yet?"

Glen just shook his head and shrugged. "She never checked in. She came in and sat on the bench for a few minutes and then left. Of course, her being alone and all, I watched to see where she went. I have to say the saloon was the last place I figured she'd end up."

"The saloon?" Panic washed over Donnell. Dolly would have his head if she heard that. He headed out the door and took off running. What had that woman been thinking, going into a saloon at night? Please let her be safe.

He pushed at the swinging doors and entered. Clarissa was just coming down the stairs. She sure had a gracefulness about her he admired.

"Mr. Kavanagh, I didn't expect to see you here so early in the day," she said. She looked tired.

"I guess I didn't expect to see you in here at all. Did you…? I mean…" Heat flooded his face. "I didn't mean to suggest you would…"

"Yes, I was given a room to stay in all by myself," she said in a cool voice. "I appreciate the hospitality I've found here. The bartender was generous enough to offer me a place to sleep. I'm grateful I didn't have to sleep outside. I do thank you for your concern, though. If you'll excuse me?" With that, she swept by him and left the bar.

Donnell followed her outside. "Wait, Miss. Plunkett. I'd like to speak with you for a moment."

She stopped and turned to face him.

"I'd like to pay for a ticket for you to go home to your family. Seeing how there isn't a groom waitin' for you here."

Her eyes narrowed. "You think I'm lying."

He opened his mouth to deny it, but she waved one hand at him. "I can tell when someone thinks I'm lying. Mr. Kavanagh, let me tell you something. I did indeed exchange letters with a Mr. Joe Kingsley, and he sent me a ticket. I have no other reason for being here. I thought about it all night, but I can't figure out what went wrong. How can I be betrothed to a man who doesn't live where he said he lived? That's the lie you need to think about." She turned and walked away. Her hips swayed in the slightest way, but he noticed.

Why hadn't he been born knowing how to be sensitive to others? "Miss Plunkett, wait." He hurried and caught up to her. "I'll investigate it all for you. I'll find out what happened. You might as well come home with me."

Her mouth opened wide, and then she snapped it closed. "Isn't that convenient? Tell me, Mr. Kavanagh, does your wife know you're here making me offers?"

"I assure you she does not," he blustered. "I mean— look, there isn't a missus. I'm not married. I live on a nice spread with my brothers. A few are married, and there are children about, and Dolly our dear housekeeper will be at the house at all times." He spoke so fast he had to take a deep breath when he finished.

Her brow furrowed as she worried her lip. "I just don't know. Truthfully, I never thought that Joe Kingsley wouldn't be here. I had hopes and dreams that relied on his promise of marriage. I suppose I could use a place to regroup. I know the saloon wasn't a moral decision, but I didn't know what else to do. It was that or sleep outside."

Donnell rubbed the back of his neck. "Do you have the letters with you? Perhaps we could look at them and see if there are any clues."

"Mr. Kavanagh, usually letters are of a personal nature. What would you be looking for?"

"Any clue that can tell us where he's from. Certain words or a mention of a town. It might help."

Her lips flattened into a tense line, but then she released a long breath and relaxed her shoulders a bit. "You're welcome to scrutinize the letters. I'm more embarrassed than angry that Mr. Kingsley wasn't here to meet me. I'll admit it was a total leap of faith, but why lure me out here and not meet me?"

They strolled along the plank walkway as they talked. "The livery is just up ahead." Donnell smiled as he gestured toward the stables. "I can rent a carriage and take you and your things out to the ranch. It'll all be entirely proper, I assure you."

"Would you mind making the arrangements while I speak again to Mr. O'Rourke at the general store? My letters were sent here."

"You solve that mystery, and I'll get everything arranged. I'll meet you at the store."

JOHN O'ROURKE TURNED his gaze to the door when Clarissa pushed it open.

She gave him a polite nod. "Good morning, Mr. O'Rourke. I was hoping to ask you a few questions."

"Good morning to you, Miss. Plunkett. I'd be happy to help." His smile didn't seem genuine to her.

"I was wondering if the letters I sent to Mr. Kingsley were here at the post office?"

"No. But if a person knew the mail stops, they could alert the driver and postmaster that the letters needed to be forwarded to a different place."

She frowned. "Does this happen to small towns or is it a Western thing? I've never heard of such a practice."

"It's the way we do it in the West," he acknowledged. "People move, especially cowboys. Some letters are just addressed to the post office or a town with a name on it. The train takes the mail to Fort Worth. After that it goes by way of stagecoaches. My best guess is either someone in Fort Worth knew to look for the letters or the stagecoach driver knew to drop the letters somewhere else. Could be the recipient of the letter met the stage somewhere. It could have been a place the stage stopped every time they came through to change horses and drivers." He offered a shrug that said he didn't much care. "I wish I had a better answer for you. Sometimes the mail official will ask if a person still lives here, and if not they take the letter with them back to Fort Worth unless someone alerts them along the way that a person's mail is to be delivered to a different place. I'm telling you it can be one colossal headache."

"I'm sorry to put you to such a bother," she apologized. "I had no idea how it all worked. It's easy enough to see why letters seem to take so long to get to the rightful person. I will be at the Kavanagh ranch if anyone should inquire."

"I'm sorry as can be about your groom, Miss Plunkett. It seems downright rude." This time his smile seemed a bit more genuine. "You take care, now."

"Thank you, Mr. O'Rourke." She stepped outside. There wasn't a way to find Joe. Had something happened to him? He must have intended to live in these parts. That was where the ticket had brought her. His letters had been sweet, and she'd trusted him. When would she ever learn that trust had to be earned and not given so lightly? It was too hard to accept that he had no intention to marry her or even meet her. Maybe he had seen her and walked away. That scenario sounded the most logical.

This entire journey had been a bust. Going to stay at a ranch was crazy. She didn't know the Kavanaghs. But she didn't see where she had any alternative at the moment. She hadn't had much choice but to leave Philadelphia, either. Her mother had never wanted her. Therefore, she had been raised by teachers at boarding schools. When she'd graduated, there was no one in the audience. Always a saver, she'd saved every bit of money her mother sent. Clarissa didn't need much. After graduation, she'd traveled back to be with her mother.

She had possessed one envelope from her mama with a return address on it. The rest of them were blank in that spot. It had been nerve racking taking a train to Bent, Texas. She'd stopped at a hotel, gotten a room and freshened up before she went to her mother's address. Her thoughts drifted back.

Music could be heard before she'd reached the building. Thatcher Saloon was written on the sign that was nailed above the door. Her heart fell. She didn't understand. Her mother had always written they'd be together once Clarissa graduated. Well, she had finished school, and now here she was. But this couldn't be the correct address. She started to turn when a tall, unshaven man ran out of the building.

"You're the very image of Irene," he exclaimed excitedly. "What an expert money maker. No one could compete."

Clarissa stiffened. "I'm sure I don't know what you mean, sir."

He laughed. "Sir, that's a good one. For all I know I could be your father but from the look of you, you could be Hank's.

Of course, there's no way to know for sure. Looking to step into her shoes, are you?"

"I must be at the wrong place. If you'll excuse me—" She glared.

He'd gripped her arm, not too tightly but tight enough it got her attention. "If you were lookin' for your ma, you have the right place. I'm so sorry to tell you she died two months ago. Stabbed she was. It was an awful thing. It's just as well, though. She had some idea she could leave here and buy a small house for the two of you. I bet you're looking for work. Come on inside and I can tell you more about your ma." He tried to guide her through the batwing doors.

Her brain had a hard time making sense of what he was saying, but she if she went through those doors she might never come back out. She yanked her arm away and ran down the street, turned, ran again, and turned once more before she leaned her back against the brick of a building. Catching her breath was near impossible as tears streamed down her face.

Her mother was…was a whore? Clarissa felt cold. Her entire life had been a lie? There wasn't a dress shop or a house? Her father was unknown? That made her a… She bent over, sick to her stomach. *Oh Mama, why?*

Why did a whore's daughter need a fancy education? With frenzied haste, she had made her way back to the hotel and ran up the stairs to her room. She'd locked the door and then jammed the back of a chair up under the doorknob. No one would be able to get to her.

She had climbed onto the bed and curled up into a ball, struggling to make sense of her life. What about the plans they'd made for after her graduation? Mama had written they'd spend all their time together. But there wouldn't be a time, whether her mother was dead or not. She'd lied about it all. The thought of them having a shop together was what had kept Clarissa going. There were years and years of lonely holidays, summers when she stayed mostly alone. She'd never been allowed to go with another student when invited. Her school had become her jail.

The looks of pity the teachers had given her suddenly made sense. They'd probably known. They'd known her about her mother. They'd heard her talk about the shop often enough, what they must have thought. All she'd ever wanted was a genuine hug from someone who loved her. Over the years she'd become withdrawn. She was fine, or so she had thought. When she had discovered the truth, her heart had broken into smaller pieces that would take forever to heal. If they ever would.

Clarissa had yearned to have friends, but something had held her back. She'd been right on the mark about that, hadn't she? Maybe all along some part of her had suspected the truth. She'd had a few girls she spent time with, but she'd never gotten close to them.

"Miss Plunkett? Clarissa?"

She shook off her musings to find Donnell standing in front of her, regarding her with one eyebrow cocked in question.

"I'm ready to go," she responded. She could do this. She wasn't a shrinking violet.

He helped her into the carriage. "Your things are in the back."

"Thank you." She tried to be outwardly confident, but inside she quaked. He had brothers. She'd never been around many men, and certainly not young ones. Luckily, they wouldn't find her very pleasing. Being plain suited her just fine; she could blend in and be forgotten about.

CHAPTER TWO

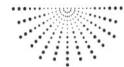

She sure didn't seem to be one for gabbing, and Donnell liked that about her. He'd help her get on her way as soon as he figured out what was really going on. He certainly didn't discount the possibility she was lying about the entire thing. His mother had lied to him his whole life. Some women were experts at it.

The steady clop of the horses was growing monotonous, though. "What did John have to say?" He finally broke the silence between them.

"I learned a lot about mail delivery," she said in a resigned tone, "and how, if you know a postal officer, you can possibly have your mail delivered anywhere no matter what the address is." She released an exasperated sigh. "It doesn't seem right to me, seeing what happened. There are many young women who want a fresh start or have nowhere to go. I can tell you the world isn't friendly if you don't have money."

Silence fell over them again.

"I appreciate you taking me to your ranch," she said after a moment. "I feel a bit awkward. I've been away at a boarding school for girls and I don't know what to say to young men. I'm afraid your brothers will find me awkward."

He couldn't contain his soft chuckle. "I wouldn't worry about it. Dolly will take excellent care of you, and some of my brothers have wives and children," he said gently. What else was there to tell her? She'd be fine? After all, she traveled by herself. He'd hand her off to Dolly, and then his part would be done. He loved a good mystery, but she was keeping something secret, and he'd had a lifetime of secrets. He would, however, make sure she was who she said she was. He couldn't put his family in danger.

"It's such a pretty spring day." She made a broad gesture toward the prairie. "What are those blue flowers?"

He smiled. They were carpeted all around Texas. "Texas Blue Belles. I'm always glad to see them. It's like they're making an official announcement that winter's over. Spring doesn't last long around here." He glanced at the clear blue sky above. "It'll be mighty hot in a few weeks."

She continued to watch the scenery. "I'm sure most places are hot in the summer. It just takes getting used to is all."

His lips twitched. "There's hot, then there's Texas hot. You'll see soon enough if you stay in these parts for long." He released a sigh. "Look, I'll see about finding Joe Kingsley for you. He might have a perfectly good excuse."

She turned toward him. "Please don't. There must be some reason he didn't meet me, and I'd never survive the humiliation of him telling me I'm not good enough."

"Why would anyone ever think you're not good enough? You're educated and you seem nice enough. And you're graceful." He swallowed. He hadn't meant to say so much.

She peered at her lap. "Thank you for saying so."

Huh. She really thought she wasn't good enough. Some of his brother's wives had been prone to quirks like that. Didn't people raise their daughters to be confident in themselves? It was a shame, really. Confidence was attractive.

"Do you have family in, um, where did you say you were from?"

"I attended The Academy for Girls outside of Pittsburg, Pennsylvania. I graduated this year and found that my mother was dead. She'd told me my father died when he was thrown from a horse." She stared into the distance, but Donnell didn't think she was looking at the bluebonnets any longer. "I gazed at the sea of people at the graduation ceremony and tried to find my mother, but she wasn't there. She hadn't come. So, I went to the only address I had for her and was told she'd been killed. She must have spent her life working to pay for my schooling. We were going to open a dress shop." When she looked back at him, a tear trailed down her face. She quickly dashed it away with her hand and went back to watching the scenery.

He was full of questions. Something wasn't right, something about her story was off. But she looked a bit wrung out. She'd probably spent the last few days finding out her world had turned upside down. Or perhaps she was a waif and was conning him. She was educated, but that didn't mean anything. He liked her but he'd been wrong before.

"Where are we?" she asked after a bit. "How long until we get to your place?"

"We're already on Kavanagh land. We have been for the past twenty minutes or so. It's a cattle ranch mostly, but we have all kinds of animals. Last I heard Sheila was trying to fix a Blue Jay's wing. She's my brother Sullivan's wife. Everyone will be on their best behavior."

As he turned the carriage into the drive, he sighed at the sight of two men rolling around in the dirt. He'd end up eating his words. He stopped Rascal and tied off the reins. "I'll be right back."

Amid shouting and a cloud of dust, Murphy and Fitzpatrick scuffled, pushing and punching each other. Fitzpatrick landed on his back, and Murphy leaped on him, getting in a good sock to the nose, which earned a savage growl from Fitzpatrick as he rolled and jumped into a crouch, fists clenched.

Donnell stalked across the distance to his brothers. "What's going on?"

Sullivan leaped off the porch and grabbed Murphy while Donnell held Fitzpatrick back.

"What is wrong with you two?" Sullivan ground out.

Fitzpatrick wiped the blood from his nose with the back of his hand. "I told that girl stealer to leave Martha alone. I saw her first!"

"All I did was talk to her," Murphy snarled. "It's not my fault she asked me onto her front porch for a glass of water!"

"You sat with her for nearly an hour! Did you propose?" Fitzpatrick asked.

"Murphy, were you sweet-talking Martha?" Sullivan asked.

"Heck no! She doesn't know one horse from another. She thinks all cattle are the same too and doesn't like to talk about ranching. What would I do with a girl like her?" Murphy glared at Fitzpatrick.

"I guess I made a mistake." Fitzpatrick's words could hardly be heard.

"You'll need to speak up, Fitzpatrick," Donnell told him.

"I'm sorry!" Fitzpatrick walked away.

"Who's the pretty gal in the carriage?" Murphy asked, peering over Donnell's shoulder.

"None of your business," Donnell said as he straightened his clothes. He walked to the carriage and helped Clarissa down. "Sorry about that. It's usually much quieter around here."

She looked into his eyes and smiled. "Your brothers I take it?"

"Yes, Murphy and Fitzpatrick. Sullivan is the one who helped to break it up."

She followed him into the ranch house. As usual, he found Dolly in the kitchen. After she finished stirring a pot of something on the stove, she turned and smiled. He made introductions and left Clarissa in Dolly's care.

"You heading out again?" Sullivan asked him.

"I have some questions I need answers to," he answered, saying as little as he could get away with.

"CLARISSA, PLEASE HAVE A SEAT," Dolly offered as she gestured to the nice furniture in front of a rather enormous stone fireplace.

"Thank you." Clarissa sat in one of the plump chairs.

"Let me get the tea and I'll introduce you to everyone. I have to confess we were pretty sure Donnell would bring you back, so we have a bit of a crowd."

As nervous as she was, Clarissa relied on all the etiquette classes she'd had, sitting up straight and smiling. "May I be of any help?"

"That's sweet," said Dolly, shaking her head. "But I can manage. I'll be right back."

Dolly carried in a sizeable tea service with several cups. She set it down on the large table in the middle of the seating area. A lovely woman with brown hair and blue eyes followed with a tray full of desserts.

Clarissa didn't have many expectations, but this was much more than she'd have imagined tea in the west to be. Donnell mentioned a few wives and children, and there were more than expected.

Dolly fixed Clarissa her tea and handed it to her. The other women sat down.

"Clarissa, this is Gemma, Heaven, Ciara, and Sheila. Gemma is married to Teagan, the oldest, and the sweet girl over there playing blocks is their daughter Lacey. Heaven is married to Quinn and they have Tim, Daisy, and Owen, the little one playing with Lacey. Ciara is married to Brogan and they have twin girls who are being looked after by their Aunt Orla. Sheila is married to Sullivan and they have Becca, the pretty girl watching over the little ones, and they also have one on the way. Don't worry, we don't expect you to remember all the names."

"I'm delighted to meet you all. My, what a big family you have."

"Do you have family close to here?" Heaven asked.

Clarissa smiled at the beautiful blond woman. "I don't. I recently found out that my mother died a few months ago."

"I'm sorry to hear that," Sheila said. She touched the back of her brown hair as though to be sure it was still in place.

"That's too bad. Is that when you decided to become a mail-order bride?" Gemma asked. She'd been the one helping Dolly.

Clarissa smiled at the stunning woman with blue eyes. "Yes. I never gave it a thought before."

"Many women are taking that step these days," Ciara remarked.

"Unfortunately, a woman's choice is limited. It is a bit scary, though," Clarissa said with a frown. "I kept hoping that Mr. Kingsley was an honest man, but I don't know. It's a mystery that left me homeless. I appreciate your hospitality."

Dolly smiled at her. "I thought the house across the way would suit your needs. You're welcome here anytime, and of course we'd love to have you for all meals. I'd keep you here in the house if there was a free room."

Clarissa's eyes grew moist for a moment. "Thank you."

"I'll have someone open the place up. It hasn't been used in a while."

Dolly was everything Clarissa had ever wanted in a mother. Everything she imagined her mother to be. But her mother had lied to her, strung her along. She supposed she had figured something was wrong when the vague promises of going home on the holidays always ended up with an excuse for why she had to stay at the school instead. Shame washed over her. Her mother must have paid extra to have Clarissa kept there.

It was a good school with a good reputation. Still, there were plenty of times when she'd felt imprisoned by the high walls that surrounded the school. Often, she had longed for just a day away, time to explore and feel some freedom. Then she'd chastised herself for her uncharitable thoughts.

As they all sipped tea, Clarissa pretended to listen and she smiled and nodded to the women. But her thoughts were miles away. Her mother had told her that her father was dead, but she now knew that she didn't have a father. Thinking about it made her feel less of herself.

Had her mother ever intended to tell her the truth? Clarissa had a drawing of her mother that had been sent to her. She did look very much like her. Her mother had never shown much interest in Clarissa's features nor had she seemed to care about her likes and dislikes. Most of her letters were brief, hoping that school was going well and Clarissa was being an obedient girl. At the time she'd been so grateful for a letter she never noticed how impersonal they were.

Her musings were once again interrupted when Dolly stood and went into another room. When she came back, she had her hands full of linens. "Follow me Clarissa, we'll get the house aired out."

Clarissa stood. "It was so lovely to meet you all. I hope we get to know each other better in the coming days."

She heard a few calls of "you too" as she walked out the door and relieved Dolly of half her load.

They entered a quaint house. It was well made and even had a stove. "It's so nice!" exclaimed Clarissa with delight. "I suppose I thought since no one else lived here it was drafty or something."

Dolly chuckled. "Most have homes of their own, some live in the bunkhouse and a few in the main house. Donnell will be back in a bit. He went to town to ask some more questions about your groom."

"How did you know where he went?"

"Murphy snuck in the back way, looking for something sweet. He told me."

"I see. I will get a job, I promise. I insist on paying you rent." She tried to sound positive, though her stomach was tying itself in knots. The rent for such a pleasant house was probably much more than she could afford.

"Don't you worry about a thing. Everything will get sorted out," Dolly said as she opened the last shutter. "Now it's a bit dusty, but other than that I'd say it was in good shape."

"It certainly is," Clarissa choked out.

"Oh dear, I've upset you."

Clarissa shook her head. "No, it's just that you are so kind and caring. It's heart expanding. Thank you."

Dolly hugged her. "I'll have one of the boys bring your things in. Supper is usually around five, depending on the sun. If the sun is up longer, supper is later. I'll see you at the house soon." She bustled out the door, and Clarissa watched her until she disappeared inside the main house.

Her days had always been so structured. School and school life ran on a tight schedule. It felt strange to stand idle and look out a window. What would Donnell find out? Did Joe Kingsley even exist? She never imagined that her groom would be a no show. Maybe this was a known risk that brides took. Frankly, she didn't know all that much about the world.

Grabbing one of the dust cloths on the dining table, she set about dusting.

CHAPTER THREE

*D*onnell stood on the front porch watching the shadows through the windows of the house Clarissa was staying in. He wasn't sure what to do with his anger short of punching one of his brothers. Especially Murphy and Fitzpatrick. Throughout supper they had acted as though Clarissa was a prize to be won. Didn't they realize she had feelings?

Clarissa didn't say much while she was at the main house. She looked decidedly uncomfortable with a plastered smile on her face. He could tell she was nervous as she walked inside though she returned his smile easy enough.

It wasn't until they sat around the table and Murphy and Fitzpatrick vied for the empty chair next to her that suppertime started to go drastically wrong. Fitzpatrick won and gloated about it. Murphy made snide remarks about Fitzpatrick all evening. Clarissa had eaten little. Her face was beet red and Donnell knew she was getting kicked under the table by his brothers.

Finally, Donnell stood and offered her his hand, which

she took. He guided her to the sofa near the fireplace. "I think coffee in front of the fire would be nice."

She nodded and then she squeezed his hand and whispered, "Thank you."

"My brothers are naïve fools," he told her softly. "How did you like the house?"

"It's grand and I really like it. Do you think I could try my hand with the flower garden? I've never— I've hardly ever been in a garden before."

He grinned. "Sheila will help you. She can make anything grow."

"I'll ask her tomorrow. Thank you." She stared into the fire.

"I know it can be chaotic with so many people and their children here, but you'll feel like one of the family in no time."

"After I marry either Murphy or Fitzpatrick?" Her smile didn't reach her eyes.

He gave a soft chuckle. "No marriage required. Besides, you're already promised."

She frowned. "Yes, you are right about that. I will take a raincheck on the coffee." Suddenly she stood and practically flew out the door.

Donnell got up, glared at his brothers, and took a cup of coffee outside with him. She wasn't taking the whole no-show groom thing well.

He leaned against the porch railing and watched her house. Hopefully, she'd get a good night's sleep. She probably hadn't gotten much sleep above the saloon last evening.

And she'd better not have bruises on her shins. He'd been kicked under the table twice, and he wasn't happy about it. He had politely pretended it wasn't happening, but he should have taken his two brothers to task and made them apologize.

Near as he could tell, Joe Kingsley was mining. He apparently decided to give it all up and start a family, but he found a sizable nugget and hasn't left since. He'd wait for confirmation on that information before he told her.

Clarissa checked the doors and shutters before she got ready for bed. The first few grades at the Academy the girls wore uniforms, but after that they were free to wear conservative dresses. Her mother had sent her many and Clarissa had assumed her mother had made them. Perhaps she did. The dress shop had been nothing but a dream that more than likely her mother had never planned to follow through on. But Clarissa had taken any extra classes that taught sewing and needlepoint. She could even make the finest of lace.

She had sewn with pride and the hope that her mother would praise her efforts. Few girls at the school had encouraged her. They didn't need to make their own clothes. They'd never need to know how to sew. It had never bothered her. Her excitement and commitment to her dream was all that had counted.

She put on her nightgown that she had made herself, of a heavyweight material. The same all the girls at the Academy had worn. She washed her face and brushed her hair exactly one hundred strokes. Then she examined herself in the mirror. Could people tell by looking at her she wasn't quality? Maybe there was something wrong with her character that she couldn't detect which made people think it was fine to abandon her? She wasn't a great beauty, but she wasn't ugly. She'd told Joe Kingsley she was plain, and he said it didn't matter to him. There was still hope that he'd been delayed though the fact no one knew him was troubling.

She carried herself with grace and confidence as she was

taught. Well, not always with confidence, but she tried not to show her fears when they seemed overwhelming. She couldn't stay here long. It would impose on the kind people's generosity, and that was never a good thing. After opening her trunk, she took out the ribbon-tied packet of letters. There weren't many, but she'd kept everything Joe had sent. She took them to bed with her and after she climbed under the covers, she untied the yellow ribbon.

Still, after reading them and re-reading them, there was nothing in any of the letters that gave her the smallest of clues where her intended husband was. He sounded honest, and he'd written that he wasn't poor, but he wasn't rich either and that suited her just fine. Why send a ticket if he had no intention of marrying her?

Where would she go from here? She needed a plan or at least a goal. Securing a job would be best, and once she'd saved enough, she'd open the store that had always been her dream. She purposely wasn't adding marriage to her goal. If she could live in the store, then she could probably do well. Yard goods could be costly, but just how costly depended on what type.

She put the letters back in their envelopes and tied them once again with the yellow ribbon. Sighing, she put them away, got back into bed, then turned down the flame in the lantern. It wasn't her oil to burn; she put the flame out.

Sleep didn't come easily. Her mind swirled with all that she'd learned, and it left her with so many doubts. Why did she always take what others did and put them on herself? Her mother's lies weren't her fault, yet she felt shamed by them. Joe Kingsley rejecting her or whatever happened, she somehow made it her fault. She'd always been that way. Tomorrow she'd get out her Bible. She liked to read the psalms. They soothed her.

The next day, Quinn entered the barn and nodded at Donnell. "Everything all right with you? You look like someone ruffled your feathers."

Donnell gave him a quick smile. "I bet I do at that. Joe Kingsley found a bit of gold and decided he didn't need a wife, but then he wanted to see what she looked like so he hid to see her get off the stage. She wasn't good enough for him. Those were his exact words, according to some of his friends I talked to. She wasn't good enough for him. He said he could afford a beautiful wife now. A couple of them offered to take her." He ground his teeth. "I knew about the gold strike yesterday but not about him seeing her."

"I'm better off without him," Clarissa said from the barn door. "He's a man who doesn't keep his word." The pain in her blue eyes made him inwardly flinch.

"I'm sorry, I should have told you before discussing it with Quinn."

She shrugged. "This is where you live. You can do whatever you like. If you'll excuse me." She turned, lifted her dress a bit, and ran back to the house.

Donnell groaned. "I guess I don't have to worry about telling her. I'll send a wire to where she said her mother had lived. Maybe she has relatives."

"She certainly needs comfort, and if she has family all the better," Quinn agreed. "I feel bad for her. I'd like to shake Kingsley."

"Shaking would only be a start," Donnell said. They grinned at each other. They'd always had each other's backs. "I'd best go see if she's all right."

He meandered on his way to the little house, trying to figure out what to say. He couldn't think of any one thing to help her feel better. Before he knew it, he was at the front door. After drawing a deep breath, he knocked.

When she opened the door, her eyes were red from crying. Without saying a word, he walked in and took her into his arms. She sobbed hard against his chest as he rubbed her back. How long did women cry? Would she be done soon? Maybe he should have left her alone. No, it was probably a good thing he was here. Now what? It felt especially nice to hold her.

He guided her to the settee and sat her down while keeping his arm around her. She seemed to calm a bit.

"You're right about a man who doesn't keep his word," he said gently. "Trust is scarce. I used to be the trusting sort, but I'm not like that anymore. I hate being suspicious of people, but if your own parents would lie to you than who can you really trust?"

She looked into his eyes as though she was searching for something. She put her head on his shoulder.

It surprised him. She didn't ask him questions.

SHE LIFTED her head but couldn't bring herself to look at him. She'd made a fool out of herself. How could Joe Kingsley reject her and not give her money to return home? Not that she had a place to return to, but it was beyond vile that the man had trapped her out here. Deep down she had hoped the girls at school had been wrong about her being so plain. But the truth was the truth, and she couldn't change it.

"I'm sorry. I shouldn't have subjected you to my outburst of tears." She squared her shoulders with bravado she didn't feel. "I try to ignore things people say, but this was different. I came all the way out here to be that man's wife. He didn't feel any responsibility toward me at all. He was probably in the saloon when I had to go in and ask for a room."

"I'm sorry you've been through so much." He gave her should an encouraging squeeze.

She stood up. "It's not proper to have you here. I'm sure enough rumors are being said without adding entertaining men alone in this house," she said, forcing a smile to temper her words. "I'm fine. Thank you though for checking on me. I need to come up with a plan for my future. Marriage is out; I'll never put myself through that again. I'll just have to save enough money to make my first dress and hopefully sell it to make a few more dresses I can sell."

"Someday you'll have your own shop," he assured her with confidence. "You have enough determination to do it. But you're right, I'd best go. Take care." Offering a polite nod, he showed himself out.

She would put on her *everything was fine* face. She'd had more than enough practice over the years. Joe's words had cut deep, and they'd brought her low. Now that she knew for certain he would not be coming for her, she had no business staying on the ranch. They had only offered her a place because they felt sorry for her. Maybe she should see about a teaching job. She had more than enough education. And at least the town wouldn't have to worry about her getting married and quitting. She could make dresses in her spare time.

Tomorrow she'd go to town and see what opportunities she could find. There had to be something. She was risking whatever reputation she had left by staying here. And she refused to play the humiliating game Murphy and Fitzpatrick seemed to be playing. They had no interest in her. They only wanted to one up the other.

CHAPTER FOUR

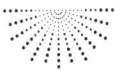

*B*y the next day, it was clear her trip to town had to wait. Dolly arrived bright and early to help with her garden, bringing Donnell along to turn the soil over for them first.

He had not looked pleased, but he worked quickly. Clarissa stole peeks at him as he worked, marveling at the easy way he lifted and turned the dirt. His muscles strained against his shirt. He must have done a lot of hard work in his life. He gave her sweet smiles whenever he caught her staring. He finished. "Have fun ladies," he tipped his hat to them both.4

Dolly was good company. "They had vegetable gardens at that school you went to?"

"They did, but we weren't supposed to get dirt under our fingernails. There was a greenhouse, and the gardener taught me so much. Then during school vacations, I always stayed behind at the Academy and I'd spend hours in the garden."

"You didn't go home?" Dolly's brow furrowed.

"No. I got many letters but never a visit, and there was always a reason I couldn't go home. I have to admit there were times I resented my mother. I was a very lonely girl. It didn't help I was one of the smallest girls. It made me feel... I don't know, inferior maybe. Silly, I suppose. But I had a roof over my head, plenty of food, and I received an excellent education." She gave Dolly a big smile. "I always counted my blessings. I knew school wouldn't last forever."

"I'm sorry. It must have been hard. I'm glad you're here. Donnell needs someone."

Clarissa opened her eyes wide. "Needs someone for what?"

"He needs a woman in his life." Dolly continued to plant seeds. "I was hoping there was interest on both sides."

"Both?"

Another seed went into the soil. "I see the way Donnell looks at you."

"Dolly, I think you're seeing something that isn't there. Donnell has been very helpful and kind, but he, we hardly know each other. I'm not entirely sure he's the type that you could push into marriage." Shaking her head, she released a sigh. "I'm going into town soon to find a job."

"I'd hoped you felt the same way he did." Dolly patted her hand. "Don't worry about it. Someone will come along for Donnell." With that, she dropped the subject of Donnell, much to Clarissa's relief.

For the rest of the day, Clarissa couldn't get Dolly's words out of her head. Donnell had been more than kind, and he was so handsome. But he didn't have an interest in her, let alone any feelings for her. He had comforted her... Dolly must be mistaken.

After cleaning the house, Clarissa sat. Never before had she just sat with nothing to do. Usually she was doing schoolwork, reading, or sewing. Just sitting gave her a lot of time to think. Dolly was nice and Clarissa really liked spending time with her. Before she'd left, Dolly had reminded Clarissa that she was to take her meals at the main house. But she truly didn't feel right about that. People often offered things just to be polite. What if she walked in and they stared at her? What if someone asked why she was there?

She paced back and forth. When she had made the decision to be a mail-order bride, she'd thought herself brave, but now she didn't feel that way. What Joe had said about her appearance wasn't news to her, but she had never heard it from a man before. The words had a truthfulness about them; he hadn't said it to be mean.

She stopped in front of the mirror and studied herself critically. Her dress was clean with no wrinkles. Her hair was pulled back nice and tight as she had been taught. Her face was washed. Her eyes were void of happiness. A sigh slipped out. She definitely had the face of a spinster. Rather than wait for a husband to leave her, she'd stay unmarried. Going to town had to be on her list for the next day. She needed to get started on her first dress.

She poured the contents of her reticule onto the table and carefully counted the coins she had left. Just enough for a dress if the material wasn't too expensive. But that meant she definitely had to keep eating with the Kavanagh family or she would end up very hungry.

If her plan came to fruition, though, she eventually wouldn't need the vegetables she planted. She'd have her dress shop with living quarters above it. She didn't need to eat much. Oh, how she missed her mother. It was supposed to be the two of them making dresses and selling them. Part of her was furious about the deception and the rest grieved for her mother, the relationship they'd never had and the death of her dreams.

How would she have handled knowing her mother was a prostitute when she was still in school? The fear of the others finding out would have been overwhelming. Life had been hard enough most times. Knowing her mother sold herself would have destroyed Clarissa.

She glanced out the window and saw Donnell walking toward her house. Dolly must have made him come to get her for supper.

Sighing, she grabbed her wrap and whisked out the door. "You didn't need to come for me."

He grinned. "Oh yes I did. That is, if I planned to eat."

"Dolly?" she asked as they walked toward the main house.

"Yes, she has deemed me to be your friend while you are here." He smiled down at her.

"I'm so sorry." Humiliation rushed warmth to her face. "I was thinking... I can go to the gold mining camp and look for Joe. I know he thinks me ugly, but maybe I can get him to live up to his responsibilities. You shouldn't be stuck with me."

He stopped and was quiet as if trying to find the right words. "I... I don't think that would be wise. Too many things could go wrong and you'd end up hurt."

"Wrong?" She tilted her head.

He shuffled his feet. Redness crept into the tips of his ears. "Most of the women in the camps are... well they're soiled doves. If he decided he still wasn't ready to marry, it could be your fate to become one of them."

"A prostitute," she murmured.

"It's a rough crowd, and it's more than likely you won't find any kindness."

"I'll put that idea to the end of the list."

A sigh whooshed from his lips. "Good. C'mon, we'd best get inside before Dolly comes looking for us."

Clarissa resisted his tug forward. "Donnell? I'm sorrier than you know that they put the responsibility of me on you. I'll live a quiet life so you don't need to worry about me."

He opened the door without responding. Had he even heard her? They walked into the kitchen, and the grins she saw on every face mortified her. Her steps faltered; she didn't know what to do. Donnell took her wrap and gave her hand a quick squeeze. A pleasing chill went through her as she followed him to the table. They were seated together again.

She joined in on the conversation at first, but the way the brothers looked at each other with a wink thrown in here and there, made her stomach churn. Did they really believe that she and Donnell… that they would become a couple? All because he'd been the one to look after her? Dread filled her. She bet he didn't like the way his brothers were acting. She ignored them.

Did people look at her differently because she was a mail-order bride? Did they think her desperate or lacking in morals? She ate slowly. She was lucky to be here, and she was very grateful. Especially when she considered the alternative Donnell had told her of when she had suggested seeking out Joe in the mining camps. If she stayed away from Donnell, they could eat in peace.

Purposely she didn't mention her need to go to town. She'd ridden a horse a few times, she wasn't very good at it, but she'd make it. Better to go on her own than make Donnell a target.

"Clarissa?" Gemma asked.

With a start, she realized someone must have said something that needed her to answer. Embarrassment warmed her cheeks. "I'm sorry I was wool gathering."

"It's a lot to take in, learning everyone's names and setting up in a new home."

"Was there something you asked me?" She gripped her fork until her knuckles turned white.

"I was saying your dress is beautiful."

"Oh," Clarissa smiled as she touched the bit of lace around the collar. "My mother made it for me."

"It's lovely."

"Thank you, Gemma. We used to send dress ideas to each other in our letters. It was difficult to find that she'd passed. I was under the impression she had a store, but she must have sewn where she lived."

"When did you find that out?" Dolly asked with concern in her voice.

"I graduated and traveled to the address she had given me. They told me she was dead. I didn't ask for more information, but now I wish I had. Needless to say, the address wasn't a fine home or a dress shop as I'd expected." She forced a sunny smile. "But I picked myself up and dusted myself off. I couldn't afford to stay. I decided a fresh start would be best. You know the rest."

The look of sympathy on everyone's faces had her stomach roiling. It was the last thing she needed. She didn't want to be Dolly's project or Donnell's pet to look after. They were just concerned, but she couldn't bring herself to eat another bite.

"Donnell why don't you take Clarissa on an enjoyable walk?" Dolly suggested.

A walk? Alone with him? Dolly was pushing too hard.

Her chair scraped as she pushed it back. "If you'll excuse me, I'm not feeling very well." She wanted to run in the worst way, but she kept her pace sedate. Once outside, though, she raced to her house and only stopped when she reached the door. She drew in several deep breaths and stared up at the darkening sky.

Lord, I feel like an orphan. I know You are my heavenly Father and I thank You. I don't think my plan of making just one dress will work. Lord, I need a plan. I need to know my path. I know You set my path, but could You maybe give me a little clue? I'm so out of sorts, and I just embarrassed myself in front of the Kavanaghs.

After a moment, Clarissa opened her door and went inside. What had she expected? That God would talk to her from the sky?

In a thunder of hoofbeats, a rider raced by and pulled up at the Kavanaghs. Clarissa shut the door but then went to the window to get a better look. The rider carried what looked to be a letter, and Donnell accepted. He said a few words to the rider before the rider raced away.

What on earth…?

Donnell opened the envelope and a hard stare was directed her way. Then he folded the paper and stepped inside. She took a step back from the window. What could be the matter?

DONNELL READ the telegram a few times. He had known Clarissa had been hiding something, but he hadn't thought she was a runaway. Someone named Hank Thatcher would be arriving tomorrow to take Clarissa back. He walked out onto the porch and closed the door behind him. He might as well tell Clarissa that she needed to finish her contract.

That was the problem with contracts. The contractor often got swindled by giving money to the other party before all the work was done and then the other party ran off. He'd guess she was a nanny or something like that. A tutor, perhaps?

The door opened before he knocked. He walked in, but not before he saw the stark fear in Clarissa's eyes.

She pointed to the telegram he held. "Is that about me?"

"Yes, it is. You should have told me you were on the run. Not fulfilling a contract is a crime." Irritation washed through him, and he drew a slow breath to calm himself. "I didn't pick up the slightest clue. You're good at lying, and that's where I draw the line. My parents lied and it was the worst thing to find out the truth."

"But I—"

"I'll have someone to drive you to town to meet the coach."

"Who do I have a contract with?"

"Hank Thatcher." He regarded her with a hard stare. "Ring a bell? You need to finish out your contract before you are free." He dropped the telegram on the table before he left.

That had been a near miss. Just as he was starting to enjoy her company. Yes, he was lucky he'd found out.

CHAPTER FIVE

*C*larissa stood on the wooden walkway in front of the general store, waiting for the coach. Murphy had taken her there in a wagon. He didn't talk to her the entire ride into town.

Shame filled her. His entire family thought her a liar. No one had been around to say goodbye, not even Dolly. They were so quick to judge. No one asked for her side of the story or even asked if she knew this man, Hank Thatcher. A shudder rippled through her. This had something to do with Thatcher's Saloon. What had Donnell told them about her? She hadn't slept all night. How could Thatcher have a contract with her name on it? Had her mother had a contract? Did he mean for her to finish out her mother's indenture? How did it all work?

The coach was due any time, and then after changing horses it would go back the way it came. She wanted to march over to the sheriff's office and tell him… tell him… Tell him what? That her mother was a whore and the man she worked for was going to force her to be one? Who would believe that? Thatcher would say *she* was the whore. No, it was better they think she ran away than think she was a whore.

The swaying black coach thundered into town and stopped right in front of where she stood. Her stomach clenched as she waited for the door to open. She'd asked the Lord for a clue, and this must be it. Terrible things happened to decent people all the time. It was her turn.

A tall, powerfully built man with overlong blond hair stepped down onto the walkway, his black boots shiny even with miles of travel behind him. He was dressed in an expensive suit with a city hat, and he held a fancy polished cane with silver glinting in the handle. As soon as he saw her, he smiled. His eyes were the same color blue as hers.

But… this wasn't the man who had met her at the saloon when she had sought her mother. Who was he?

"I finally found you, my sweet Clarissa!" he said in a rich, deep voice.

"I-I'm sorry, I don't know who you are…"

"Hank Thatcher, my little one." He touched the brim of his hat. "I'm here to collect you and take you home. It'll take but a moment, and we'll probably be on our way."

"We'll eat something first," the driver said over his shoulder.

Thatcher offered his arm to her, and she knew she didn't dare refuse. "A nice respite will be pleasant. Come along, my sweet."

Swallowing hard, she allowed him to escort her to a small diner. He held her chair out for her, took off his hat and laid it along with his cane on the empty chair next to him.

"I've been looking all over for you. Mike never should have let you get away."

"Mike?" she asked, confused.

"Mike Pinny. The man you met at my establishment," explained Mr. Thatcher. "He used to run the place for me until I fired him."

"Oh…" She'd thought that unshaven man had been the owner.

"Listen," Thatcher leaned forward over the table. "I need your mother's debt paid. Perhaps you didn't know about it, but it is a substantial sum. There's the question of the contract."

Clarissa shook her head. "I didn't sign any such contract."

"I drew one up while she was dying." He shrugged. "She indicated you would fulfill her obligation and she signed it. It was such a shame that you never got to meet her. You look very much like my Irene. She had you when she was very young. She wasn't even sixteen, if I remember correctly. You lived with her until you were four. Then it was school for you. Her greatest wish was to visit you, but it was never the right time." A cunning smile stretched his lips, and she shuddered. Had she really thought his eyes looked like hers? They had turned cold as ice and hard as flint.

"I need some fresh air," she said as she stood.

The waitress walked over. "Can I get you something?"

"No, not this time. Thank you kindly." Thatcher turned his shining smile on the lady as he also stood.

The waitress blushed, and Clarissa closed her eyes. Everyone bought his gentleman act. Thatcher again offered his arm. When Clarissa hesitated, he tilted his head and raised one eyebrow. Her hand shook as she settled it on his arm.

Her legs trembled as they walked to the coach and climbed aboard.

"I'm so glad it's just us. I want to get to know you much better." He leered at her.

All the blood left her face and she had to hold her hands on her lap to stop them from shaking. Surely he didn't mean... "You probably know all you need to know, Daddy."

"Daddy? I admit there is a very slim chance. A very slim one, you understand?" He shook his head and his leer deepened. "No, I want you for my own."

She smiled. "Look at my eyes. It's like looking in a mirror, isn't it? Of course you're very handsome and I'm plain, but there is no mistake. You don't need me to go back with you. You wouldn't allow your own daughter to work in such a place."

He laughed. "Of course, I would. I could make a lot of money because of your purity."

As they traveled on, she rarely spoke to him, barely acknowledged him. Fear filled her. Why would her mother sign such a vile contract?

THE SALOON WAS BIGGER than she remembered, and she stumbled as he shoved her through the swinging doors. It was late in the day, and plenty of customers filled the place.

Oh Mama, what have you gotten me into? And why?

Thatcher's glance flitted about the room until it settled on something near the bar. "Jewel, come here."

A pretty woman probably in her twenties came to him right away. "I'm so glad you're back, I missed you." She gave him a loving smile.

"Jewel, this is Clarissa. She's Irene's daughter and is going to finish out her mother's contract."

The green feathers in Jewel's hair bobbed up and down as she nodded.

"I need you to get her ready to put on display. We will have an auction in a few days."

Jewel's eyes widened. "Come along, Clarissa. Your mother's room is empty."

The stench of whiskey, beer, and unwashed bodies was overwhelming. She followed Jewel, wondering how she could run away. But running would be useless, she knew, for Thatcher would only track her down again. She wanted — needed — to see that contract.

Jewel showed her to a small room and explained many of the rules. Clarissa hardly heard her. She could only pray she would do nothing that would break the rules. Jewel brought out a few outlandish dresses and instructed Clarissa how to get ready to go downstairs.

"I'll be back in a half hour. You'd best be ready. Hank can have a heavy hand when displeased."

Clarissa nodded and waited for Jewel to leave. As soon as she was alone, she sat on the edge of the bed and cried. What must Donnell think of her? He'd called her a liar and maybe he was right since she hadn't told him everything about her mother, but she hadn't been a prostitute. She stared at the clothing Jewel had left. It was indecent. Certainly nothing a respectable lady would wear. The thought of putting it on and parading in front of the men downstairs turned Clarissa's stomach. But she would have to if she wanted to avoid Hank's heavy hand. She stood and stared at the dresses and after a bit of thought, chose a black and yellow one that her mother must have made. It had perfect tiny stitches. After she changed into it, she cringed. It showed too much of her skin. Maybe since she was so plain, no one would want her.

There was a knock on the door and before she could call out, Hank opened it and walked in. "Let's go, I want to seat you at the end of the bar for all to see. No drinking. If a man buys you a drink, the bartender knows to make yours water with just a splash of whiskey. Come along."

He led her down the stairs and lifted her onto the bar.

She'd thought she'd be sitting in a chair at the end of the bar, not on the bar itself where she was exposed for everyone to ogle. Her entire body heated. This couldn't have been what her mother had wanted for her.

CHAPTER SIX

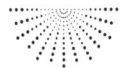

Donnell hit the wall of the barn. He didn't care about the pain blossoming in his hand. He couldn't believe he had fallen for Clarissa's friendly girl act. She must have planned to escape from Hank Thatcher for a while; being a mail-order bride and all. He couldn't even say she had dazzled him with her beauty. He'd just been stupid.

Maybe he was falling for her. There, he'd finally admitted it. He didn't mind one bit being responsible for her. She was nice and polite and didn't chatter on like some people did. Sour grapes, that's what had led to him thinking her plain. When she smiled, her face lit up and there was true beauty there. He had been so consumed by the fact that she had lied, that he never even asked what type of work she had run from. He hadn't given her a chance to say anything. What if that man, Thatcher, wasn't such a good guy?

Quickly, Donnell saddled Rascal and rode to town. He needed answers.

He tied the roan to the hitching post in front of the general store and went inside.

"John, I need to send a couple telegrams."

"Sure thing," said the shopkeeper, picking up a pencil and paper.

After he gave John the particulars of the messages he wanted to send, Donnell walked by the yard goods. A bolt of fabric in a midnight shade of blue with the smallest of white flowers on it caught his eye. It would have looked lovely on Clarissa.

The tapping of the telegraph machine signaled a message coming across, and his heart raced. Could he have gotten an answer so quickly?

With a grim expression, John handed the paper to him. Donnell read, quickly absorbing the words from the headmistress at The Academy for Girls. Clarissa had graduated from the school and had planned to meet her mother, though her mother was unsuitable. He raised his brow. What did unsuitable mean? There had been little time between graduation and her showing up here. Barely enough to correspond with that man Joe Kingsley and agree to be his mail-order bride. She looked and acted like a polished young lady, and yet she hadn't had enough money to stay at the hotel when she had arrived. Something wasn't right.

"John, I need to send another telegram. This one's going to the sheriff over in Bent.

The bartender signaled to Hank and whispered into his ear. An enormous grin crossed Hank's face.

"Well, well Clarissa, you have an extra day before the auction. Word has it a high stakes poker game is to take place here this weekend. That'll bring a lot of customers. See, you're making money already."

"Enough to pay off the debt?" she asked hopefully.

He laughed loudly. "The auction doesn't count. It's the

work you do after that'll pay off your mama's debt. If you're lucky, you might pay it off in five years."

"I don't believe you! I don't think there is a contract." Boldly she tossed the words at him but then cringed as he grabbed her arm.

"You're very lucky I need you unmarked for the auction. Generally, any whore who dares to question me gets beat." A leer slid over his face. "Now sit up and smile. The number of drinks you get the men to buy goes toward the debt."

She sat up straight and tall. "Really? How much a drink?"

"Half a penny. It adds up, but you have to pay us back for the drink you get. So half of what you make on drinks goes back to me. You'll want to eat and have a roof over your head, that costs money too. On the bright side, you have youth and purity. Shame you aren't more attractive." He shook his head.

Clarissa stared at her hands. Why bother to have her on display? She wasn't pretty enough to be a whore. Shame washed over her. Her mother must have allowed her arms and legs to be seen like this. How had she stood it? At least no one was allowed to touch her... yet.

She was smart, though. There must be a way to escape. They couldn't have guards at the door at all times. She'd watch and look for patterns. There must be a time when she could sneak out.

She lifted her head and smiled. If she acted as though she had made peace with her fate maybe Hank wouldn't watch her as closely.

The night was interminable, and the stench of cigars, whiskey and beer was enough to turn her stomach. The men who bought her drinks were a mixed bag. A few were washed and smelled clean, a few others looked dirty but didn't have a foul smell and then there were the men who probably bathed once a year. Their fetid breath was hard to tolerate, let alone smile. She'd been sitting on the bar for so long now the night must be about over.

She needed to use the outhouse but wasn't sure how to ask. Finally, she whispered her needs to the bartender, who gave her an amused smile and then signaled for Hank to come over. "She needs to use the outhouse and stretch her legs."

Hank got too close to her when he lifted her down, and she had to force herself not to stiffen. "I'll take you."

Hank opened the outhouse door and shoved her in. She trembled as she looked for any animals. Usually she was more cautious with her approach. She hurried to do what was necessary, and when she came out, she insisted on washing her hands at the well. Hank didn't seem happy, but he waited.

"How long did my mother work here?"

He shrugged his left shoulder. "It seemed like she'd always been here. She was real young. I remember you as a kid running around. Your mother was a real looker and very popular. She worked extra hard to pay for your schooling. She was always the first whore down in the afternoon and the last one still working at the end of the night."

They walked back into the raucous bar. Hank lifted her up to her spot and walked around the bar keeping an eye on the girls. Why none of the girls gave him an evil stare behind his back, she couldn't imagine. The crude way the customers spoke disgusted her.

Jewel sauntered over. "It's time to put you away for the night." She held out her hand and helped Clarissa down. "It's getting a bit rowdy in here, and Hank doesn't want anything to happen to you."

"Isn't that so sweet of him?" He just wanted her pure for the auction. Whatever the reason, she was happy when Jewel grabbed a plateful of beans and escorted her to her mother's room. The sound of the door locking when Jewel left didn't surprise her.

The light cast from the oil lamp was dim, and she turned the wick up. So, her mother had been here for at least eighteen years. Clarissa had been born in this horrible place. How had her mother made enough money to put her through school? Maybe that was most of the debt. *Oh Mama, you could have had your dream of a dress shop if not for me. I'm so sorry you had to live this way.*

She put on her heavy night gown and pushed a wooden chair up against the door. She didn't have one person she could trust, this situation was dire. Her mother had given up so much. Clarissa opened the nightstand drawer and dug through it, blinking in surprise when she lifted the frilly undergarments and found a Bible. She sighed in relief. She glanced through the Psalms and paused at Psalm five, feeling like it spoke to her. She read it repeatedly before she said it out loud again and again.

Give ear to my words, O LORD;
consider my meditation.
Hearken unto the voice of my cry,
my King, and my God:
for unto thee will I pray.
My voice shalt thou hear in the morning, O LORD;
in the morning will I direct my prayer unto thee,
and will look up.
For thou art not a God that hath pleasure in wickedness:
neither shall evil dwell with thee.
The foolish shall not stand in thy sight:
thou hatest all workers of iniquity.
Thou shalt destroy them that speak leasing:
the LORD will abhor the bloody and deceitful man.
But as for me, I will come into thy house in the multitude of thy mercy:

and in thy fear will I worship toward thy holy temple.
Lead me, O LORD, in thy righteousness because of mine enemies;
make thy way straight before my face.
For there is no faithfulness in their mouth;
their inward part is very wickedness;
their throat is an open sepulchre;
they flatter with their tongue.
Destroy thou them, O God;
let them fall by their own counsels;
cast them out in the multitude of their transgressions;
for they have rebelled against thee.
But let all those that put their trust in thee rejoice:
let them ever shout for joy, because thou defendest them:
let them also that love thy name be joyful in thee.
For thou, LORD, wilt bless the righteous;
with favor wilt thou compass him as with a shield.

BEFORE SHE FELL ASLEEP, she prayed for the Kavanagh family. They had been kind and generous. Was Donnell sleeping already?

CHAPTER SEVEN

Finally, Donnell got a message back from the sheriff of Bent. Hank Thatcher was indeed a businessman but a shady one.

He paced from one end of the barn to the other. How shady? What kind of shady? The information was vague.

"What's wrong?" Sullivan asked, looking up from the bridle he was mending.

"Clarissa. I just couldn't let it go. I had to scrutinize the situation, and I'm not happy with what I've found. The man who came to get her is some shady businessman. I don't even know what that means."

"There must be something wrong with where she's working." Sullivan crossed his arms in front of him. "What are you waiting for? That girl needs your help. Or were you waiting for a personal invitation from her? Saddle up, I'll have Dolly fix you some food, and I'll grab some supplies."

Donnell smiled. "You certainly have gotten bossy, Sullivan, but in this case you're right."

By the time Donnell got Rascal saddled and his bedroll

attached, he met up with Sullivan. "Thanks. I wanted to go, but I couldn't decide."

"Sheila changed my character. You can't control everything, but if you can act do it."

"How is she by the way? Prison must have been an ominous place."

"She's a different person too; for the better. We both grew a lot and she's finally at the point where she can relax and take things one day at a time." Sullivan finished helping tie the supplies to the saddle. "Good luck."

Donnell swung up on Rascal and rode off. All of his older brothers had gotten married and they were better men for it. He rode until dark and made camp. He wasn't going to bother with a fire but as soon as he heard the wolves howl, he thought better of it, gathered some fallen wood and lit one.

The next morning, he washed in the stream and made himself coffee. Dolly had sent enough biscuits for a week. As he chewed on one, he considered Clarissa. He should have checked into her background deeper. What was it about her that had caught him off guard? She was brave, able to take care of herself, no wilting violet, that was for sure. He admired the way she bucked up after all she'd been through.

He finished breakfast then saddled and mounted Rascal and headed off. Bent wasn't too far, maybe another three hours. Clarissa didn't need to know he was in town, in case he was wrong and she was doing well for herself. He didn't want to bring any trouble on to her. He just wanted to investigate the situation. He had too many questions and that never sat well with him.

Finally, he rode along Bent's main street. The town was bigger than he'd imagined. The place was crawling with cowboys. They must have just bought or sold cattle and were taking a bit of a holiday. Now to find the sheriff. He walked along the boardwalk and into the sheriff's office.

"Sheriff Wheat?"

The man sitting behind the desk shook his head. "I'm Deputy Polk. The Sheriff is down at Thatcher's Saloon. They're auctioning off a girl. I had to stay behind." He sounded upset about it.

Donnell frowned. "Auctioning off a girl for what?"

Deputy Polk just leered, his ominous chuckle sending chills along Donnell's spine.

He swore under his breath and left without a word. Thatcher's was at the end of the town. It was a big saloon and his stomach dropped. How could he have allowed Clarissa to be taken to a saloon? Work contracts happened all the time; he'd had no reason to think the work was in a saloon. But he hadn't bothered to find out where she was going, either.

He walked in and the place was utter chaos. People were buying tickets, so they'd be eligible to bid. He scanned all the tables, but he didn't see her. He'd ask the bartender what was going on and hopefully he could ask about Clarissa without drawing unwanted attention.

"Whiskey," he ordered.

"Would you like to buy one for our virgin?" The bartender nodded toward the end of the bar. There she sat on the bar looking frightened and exhausted.

"Do I get to talk to her?"

"Sure enough. This young crowd aren't much for talking. I mainly need to make sure no one touches her."

Donnell squared his shoulders before he went to the end of the bar. She didn't turn her head.

"This here fella bought you a drink," the bartender said with a warning in his voice.

She instantly smiled and thanked him. Her eyes widened

and he could see they were full of despair. "Hello Donnell. How are things?"

"I could ask you the same question."

"Mister if you want to keep talking you need to buy more drinks for the two of you," the bartender told him with a scowl.

"Fair enough. We'll have another and if I'm still talking pour another." He laid cash on the bar.

"How much have you had to drink?" Donnell asked her.

"Mine is mostly water. Why are you here?"

"I'm nosey. I like to know everything that's going on, and after I thought about it, the whole contract thing didn't make sense." He tilted his head and gave her a smile. "And I was worried about you."

"I appreciate your concern." She swallowed hard. He got the notion she was terrified but trying hard not to show it. "There isn't anything you can do. My mother signed a contract between Thatcher and me. From what I gather, he promises girls they can earn their way out of here, but he charges more for room and board than they could possibly pay." A cheer went up across the room, and she shivered. "The auction money doesn't count."

"Why not?"

"Thatcher said so."

"I want to see the contract," he growled.

"So do I, but he hasn't shown it to me yet. And there is no way to leave. It never occurred to me to change my name and go as far as I could. I had no reason to think anyone would hunt me down. I didn't even know Mr. Thatcher." A lone tear slipped down her face. She quickly wiped it away and glanced about as though fearful of being caught crying. After a moment, her shoulders relaxed.

"When is this auction?"

"Tomorrow around nine. Do you like my dress? My mother made it." Her voice sounded flat.

"I'm not going to answer that." He offered a gentle smile. "You may swat me if I tell you the truth. I just hate you have to wear it in front of all these men. I'll wrap my coat around you."

She put her hand up to stop him. "That would just make Thatcher angry, and he's already angry with me. He's saving his anger for after the auction. He doesn't want any marks on me until after. I've earned myself a beating, it seems." She didn't look at him but her skin had turned red.

"You'll be safe until tomorrow?"

"Yes," she mumbled.

"I'll be back before that. I've missed you."

He turned and walked to the line for purchasing a ticket to be allowed to join the auction. He finally stood in front of Thatcher. "Looks like a big turnout. If I'd known you ran auctions, I'd have come sooner."

"No, this is the first. She's special and pure."

"She's no beauty." Maybe Thatcher would change his mind.

Thatcher laughed. "Turn the lights off." All the men in line behind Donnell laughed too.

Donnell bought his ticket and went to see a lawyer he knew.

They greeted each other with a hug and a slap on the back. Donnell had always liked Leo Best. They had served together, and the dark-haired, dark-eyed man was always logical and mostly right.

"Nice office. You must be doing well." Donnell glanced around before he sat in a chair in front of Leo's desk.

"Things are going well. What about you?"

Donnell studied the man sitting across from him. "I've got a problem. It involves a woman."

"It always does." Leo chuckled.

"Clarissa Plunkett is being auctioned off at the saloon."

"The sheriff will have to take care of it."

Donnell ran his fingers through his hair. "The sheriff bought a ticket to be allowed to bid tomorrow night."

Leo sat back in his chair. "How do you know this woman?"

"She came to Huntertown as a mail-order bride, but her groom didn't want her. I saw her go into the hotel and didn't give her another thought. We found out she rented a room at the saloon and I went to bring her to the ranch."

Leo drummed his fingers on the desk. "What kind of woman is she?"

"She is shy and sometimes seems afraid. She's been helpful around the ranch, insisting she wouldn't take charity. She can be standoffish, but that might be because she's shy. She grew up in a boarding school in Pennsylvania. Her mother never visited and Clarissa never was allowed home during school breaks, so I gather she didn't really know her mother. She told me her mother was a dressmaker and they were supposed to run the store together but after graduation she came here to find her and found out her mother had died and there was no dress shop." He paused and drew a deep breath. "Then I got a telegram from a Mr. Hank Thatcher, who said she had run away before she finished her contract. Stupid of me, but I thought she was a nanny or something and just didn't want to finish her indenture."

"Have you seen the contract?" Leo asked.

Donnell shook his head. "Clarissa told me her mother signed it on her behalf. It's a contract to work for Thatcher."

"Did her mother get paid to sign?"

"No."

Leo frowned and rubbed his chin. "Did you say Plunkett?"

Donnell nodded.

"There used to be an Irene Plunkett living in town," mused Leo. "She was stabbed to death. She had been looking at a couple of empty buildings. She was opening a store is what I heard. I wonder what happened?"

"I'm going to see what I can find out today, and I want to see that contract. Do you think it's binding?"

"If the daughter was under her mother's care at the time, then unfortunately, yes. But we have to be sure it's her mother's signature. If worse comes to worst, you can try to buy out the contract."

"That gives me hope. I'll let you know if I find out anything about the contract." Donnell got up.

Leo stood as well and saw Donnell to the door. They shook hands. "It was really good to see you," Leo said.

Donnell smiled. "We'll have to catch up. Did you ever marry your Mary Ann?"

"Three years married and one son. Life has been good."

"Great to hear!" Donnell walked out onto the boardwalk. Unless what Thatcher was doing was illegal, he wouldn't be able to stop it. Would the man consider a buyout? Donnell didn't want to tip his hand too early. He had more money than he'd ever need, so that wasn't a problem though it rankled he might have to give the money to Thatcher. But if it meant he could hold Clarissa in his arms again he'd give everything he owned.

He walked to the general store. When he saw a group of men playing checkers near the front, he smiled. They probably gossiped more than any woman. He took a seat by a heavily bearded man with kind eyes who asked if he wanted to buy a cup of coffee. Donnell agreed and sat watching the checkers game going on.

"Here tell that Hank is auctioning off a girl," the bearded man said.

A thin man just nodded but an older gentleman took his pipe from his pocket and lit it.

"He claims she has to work to finish out her ma's contract," said another older man. "I don't see how that can be legal. Hank has gotten away with so much around here he now thinks anything goes."

"It's not legal, at least not in Texas. But sometimes debts have to be paid when a person dies. It's just a way of slavery, and it ain't right," the bearded man said.

"That and Hank being her pa and all."

Donnell set down his coffee cup and hurried out the door. He walked briskly to the telegraph office and sent a message telling the operator he'd wait for a reply. It took about an hour but he got his reply. It was good to have friends.

CHAPTER EIGHT

Worry had worn Clarissa out. Tonight was the night, and she hadn't seen Donnell. There was probably nothing he could do. Why did she feel worse about losing Donnell than being sold? She hardly knew Donnell. He was handsome, generous, kind. She'd never seen his heart to know how big it was. There had been too much pressure with her being his responsibility. He probably resented her, and who wouldn't? Being thrown together didn't mean a thing.

At school, she'd roomed with the same girl for years, and the girl had hardly talked to her. All the loneliness she'd endured came back and filled her anew. She supposed she had been lucky the other girls hadn't known what her mother had done for a living.

She had spent considerable time over the past few days studying Hank. The more she stared at him, the more she became convinced he was her father. He had an inkling too. One of the girls had been talking about it. That didn't matter, though, because he was still going to sell his daughter. Perhaps if she was braver, she'd have run by now.

Jewel walked into the room carrying a white dress. "Hank wants you to wear this along with these silk stockings. I hope Hank treats you better than most, bein' he's your pa and all. The only advice I can give you is to relax and think of something else. Building dreams that will never come true is all we have as an escape. Whatever you do don't embarrass Hank. He likes to think we're well trained willing to do his bidding. He'll come for you in half an hour."

Clarissa was trapped. The white dress was made of many layers of sheer material topped with an overlay lace. Still, her arms would be bare. She rolled the stockings on and secured them. After she put on the dress it shamed her that much of her legs were not covered by the dress.

Lord, I don't even know where to start. I'm going to need Your help to be brave. Sometimes fate is just fate. Please protect me from harm. You have always been the one I could talk to. No matter what You have my unwavering love and faith. It's my faith in You that makes me strong.

She was ready when the door opened, and Hank Thatcher stood in the opening wearing a new shirt and vest. The irony wasn't lost on her. *The father walks his daughter down the aisle and gives her to a man.* Except this wouldn't bring her a husband. Quite the opposite, it would make her too sullied to ever marry.

"Come along."

She walked out of the room and took his proffered arm. "Did you and Mama name me? How many other children do you have?"

He gave her a warning glance. "No, I had nothing to do with you, and as far as I'm concerned I have no children. It'll only make it harder if you fight me on this. There is no way to escape. Remember that." He walked faster hauling her along.

Finally, he dragged her up by his side and they descended

the stairs. Her heart pounded and her eyes smarted. The place was packed, and it was only the afternoon. There were all manner of men, from the obviously poor to the stuffy rich. The cowboys all staring at her didn't have a chance.

This time Hank put a chair on the bar. He climbed up and the bartender lifted her to him. He made her sit on the chair. "Don't do anything to ruin this for me." He jumped down and smiled. "Gentlemen here she is, the purest woman in the whole state of Texas. Bidding starts at nine tonight. No touching her."

From her high perch she could see the whole crowd. She looked and looked but there was no sign of Donnell. She'd demanded of Hank to see the contract herself, earning the promise of a worse beating after the auction. And now it was too late to do anything but go along with his vile plans for her. She'd had a glimmer of hope when the sheriff walked in… until he shook Hank's hand. Were the town leaders present as well? Those upstanding citizens who were probably all married.

She felt the chair wiggle. The bartender handed her a watered drink. "Pay attention. I'm busy enough without trying to get your response!" She took the small glass and drank the contents. It was cold tea. All the better, since she'd need to keep her head clear.

She was so stiff from the uncomfortable chair. It was starting to get dark, and she didn't know how they could pack another person into the saloon. Round about seven o'clock Hank had everyone with less than one hundred dollars to bid pushed out the door. She still saw toothless, grimy men in the saloon. She glanced at the bartender.

"Miners. They have lots of money."

She nodded. The waiting caused her stomach to churn. She'd been offered food, but she was afraid of getting sick.

As seven o'clock turned into eight-thirty she accepted

that Donnell couldn't help her. Her hands began to shake; this was really happening. Hank stood on top of the bar a few minutes before nine to announce the auction. It shamed her to no end to hear him describe the prize.

There was a hush as Donnell came through the door flanked by two Texas Rangers. Hank backhanded her across the face and her head felt as though it was going to fly off her neck. Then he jumped down.

"Do we have some problem?"

"Hank I'd like you to meet my friends. Texas Ranger Bilks and Texas Ranger Matthews. Behind me is my lawyer Leo Best."

"The auction is over folks!" Bilks said. A chorus of loud groans rose but many of the men left quickly.

"She's my property. I can do whatever I want with her," Hank insisted.

Donnell crossed the room and lifted her down to the floor. She wished he'd put his arms around her in comfort, but he immediately stepped away. He took his jacket off and put it around her shoulders.

"I'd like to see this contract you have," the man named Leo Best said.

Hank glared at her as he went into his office with Matthews tailing him. They came back with Hank holding on to a document. He shoved it at Leo. "All legal."

Leo took his time reading the contract. "Her mother signed it?"

"Of course she did," snapped Thatcher.

"Her mother couldn't sign for her eighteen-year-old daughter."

"I must have dated it wrong," Hank insisted.

"Slavery is over," Bilks said. "You need to come with me until we get this all sorted out. You are a low, low piece of—

excuse me ma'am." Bilks grabbed Hank by the scruff of his neck and pushed him out the door.

Ranger Matthews shook Donnell's hand. "We won't need you or the lady to testify. Got plenty of witnesses."

"I appreciate how fast you got here," Donnell said.

"We could always use a man like you in the Rangers. Anytime, just get in touch." He tipped his hat. "Ma'am I wish you all the best."

"I'll walk out with you," the lawyer said after he shook Donnell's hand.

Donnell turned toward Clarissa and cupped her face. "Did he hurt you?" An angry bruise was forming on her cheek.

She shook her head. "I'm fine. I'm going to get changed. Will you be here when I'm done?"

"I'll wait however long it takes."

She nodded and went up the stairs.

He'd take her back to the ranch and make sure she was safe. He really wanted to kiss her but the fact that she lied got to him.

He expected the truth and maybe sometimes he went too far by investigating a person's past, but he'd sworn to himself he'd never allow anyone to lie to him again. It had been a few years now and it still hurt the same as it did when he was first told Brogan was his half-brother. A product of an affair his father had with the neighbor woman who was also married at the time. After she had the baby her husband had dropped Brogan off at the Kavanagh ranch and the brothers were never the wiser for a long time. That had left him feeling betrayed and it was hard to trust.

Clarissa came down the stairs with a carpetbag in her

hands. He hurried to the bottom of the steps and took her bag from her.

"What are your plans now?" he asked.

The look of shock on her face surprised him. "I…well, I hadn't given it any thought. I never thought I'd get away from this place. Thank you for all you did. I suppose I'll wait until morning and see if there is a job available somewhere in town." She gave him a small smile before her face crumbled and she turned away.

"I'm taking you back to the ranch. You can't stay in this town. I have one condition."

"What?" She turned back and met his gaze.

"We stay as friends and only friends."

She stared into his eyes and then gave him a curt nod. "Of course. We might as well get going."

"Yes, I want to make tracks. Even the smallest distance from this town would make me feel better."

"Whatever you think is best." She walked out through the saloon doors and looked up into the night sky. "Thank you again."

"I'm afraid we'll have to ride double on Rascal. I was going to get you a horse of your own but it occurred to me you might not know how to ride." He went to Rascal's side and tied the carpetbag to the saddle.

He mounted up first and reached his hand down. "Put your foot on top of mine in the stirrup." As soon as he was able to get her off the ground, he placed her in front of him. The scent of honeysuckle floated from her hair, teasing and tempting. It almost had him thinking about a relationship with her. So he steeled his heart against her and rode out of town.

God had saved her, and His instrument was the one person she wanted to love her but he never would. Still she was very grateful. Her night could have ended much differently. She relaxed and her back touched Donnell's chest. Immediately she sat forward a bit. He didn't want a relationship. Had he meant the words to hurt? She wasn't good enough for him anyway. He'd be too embarrassed in front of his influential friends if he had to introduce her as his wife.

She'd find a good husband, though. All of the time she'd had to think in the saloon led to one conclusion. She couldn't protect herself let alone support herself. There was a shortage of women in Texas, at least that was what she'd heard. All of the men who were in the saloon were immediately eliminated.

She didn't have the luxury of time, though. Dolly might know who was looking for a husband. Now that was settled, she could think about what happened to her. She shivered.

"Are you all right?" His breath was warm on her neck.

"Yes."

"We'll stop here for the night." He rode Rascal toward some large boulders. Then he got down. He faced her and put both hands up, wrapping them around her waist. Then he set her down and quickly took a step back.

It felt like a slap in the face. There must be a way she could get a better grip on her feelings. Slowly she followed Donnell as he led Rascal behind the boulders. It was a big private patch of dirt and that was all they needed.

"I did bring two bed rolls so we can sleep apart."

She took the one he handed her. She settled her blankets and he put his at the farthest point from her. At least the dark hid her heated face. To think she'd thought he cared for her. She lay down and turned her back to him. She heard him rustling his bedroll and assumed he did the same.

When she heard his breathing become steady, she knew

he was asleep. Tears poured down her face as she put her fist into her mouth to silence her sobs.

Donnell told her he didn't put up with lies and he had made it clear he found her lies were extensive. Maybe she should have told him her mother was a… that she worked in a saloon. Thatcher's appearance with a contract had been a shock to her, and she hadn't had time to explain anything to him, especially since she hadn't known much herself. Then there was the auction. Her past had come back to haunt her and put an end to her only hope of love.

"Are you crying?" His voice jolted her.

She stiffened. "Of course not. I can't let almost being auctioned off bother me. I need to be strong." But her sniffle was sure to give her away.

"I wish…We'll be home tomorrow."

She didn't reply. After all, it wasn't her home.

"I'm sure Murphy will be happy to help you."

"Is he looking for a wife? I've decided I need to be married to be safe. I can't stay on your ranch forever, and my dress shop is just a silly dream. It's time to be practical. If Murphy isn't interested, do you know who might be looking for a wife? I want to do this fairly quickly."

"I didn't know you were looking. Is there a reason for your hurry?" He sounded suspicious.

"I just want to get on with my life. I want to be somewhere I belong. I want a husband who cares for me." She shrugged. "Of course, that may be the biggest hurdle in my plan."

"Why would you think that?" She could tell from the sound of his voice he'd turned, facing her direction."

Tears filled her eyes. "You would be the one to know." Thankfully, there wasn't a response. She worked on getting to sleep.

CHAPTER NINE

*S*tanding in the middle of the great room, surrounded by his family, Donnell's head spun. The majority of his family thought he had to marry Clarissa. They hadn't been back an hour when he'd been summoned to a family gathering. When Dolly had dropped the news that he was expected to marry Clarissa, he told them no.

One by one, his brothers had started in on him.

"Donnell, everyone knows you traveled alone together," Murphy said.

"Murphy it's none of your business. You just wait until they think it's your turn to marry and see how you like it! *I* will decide who I marry, and it certainly won't be a woman who lies," he said more heatedly than he wanted. Everyone stared at him, hard. The room had become quiet, too quiet.

He didn't turn around. He couldn't bear to look at her anymore. His heart ached too much. He stalked out the back door and down to the stream. All he had wanted to do was help her, and now he couldn't bring himself to look at her. Being in the same room was incredibly difficult. This was all

Joe Kingsley's fault. If that man had met his bride when she came to town none of this would have happened.

He kicked at the muddy bank. He would have helped even if he hadn't known her. No one deserved to be auctioned off. She'd been nothing but trouble from the first. Hard work helped. He stomped to the barn and got Rascal ready to ride the range.

He stopped after riding for a while. There was a fence to fix. He hated having fences. Used to be you could trust your neighbors. He swore the bullet hit before he even heard it. The pain in his thigh was fading. It must be the adrenaline. Either that or he was dying. He stayed on the ground with his pistol in his hand.

He waited for a long while, playing dead. Rascal kept nudging him. The pain was coming back in force. He had to get on Rascal before he was unable. It wasn't easy but he eventually sat in his saddle. He didn't have to direct Rascal; he knew the way. Who had shot him? Good thing they weren't a better shot or he'd be dead. Rascal didn't stop at the barn, he took Donnell to the front door of the house and kicked at the railing on the steps.

He'd waited long enough. No one had come to the door. Just as he got ready to fall onto the ground, the door opened. He heard Dolly scream and then the world went black.

SULLIVAN and his wife Sheila tended to him. They removed the bullet and Sullivan sewed him up.

Clarissa felt helpless and out of place. She didn't know where things were. Useless that's what she was. She wanted to brush Donnell's hair back off his face and hold his hand. It was hard to pretend he didn't matter to her.

When they were done bandaging him up, Teagan and

Quinn carried him upstairs. She couldn't think of a single reason she could give to see him.

Brogan and his pretty wife, Ciara ran inside each holding one of their twin girls. Their eyes were wide as they glanced around.

"I can take care of Brigid and Tamsin," Clarissa offered as she pulled a crate of toys into a quiet corner.

"Thank you." Brogan set Tamsin on the floor first, and then Ciara placed Brigid next to her sister ever so gently.

Clarissa smiled as she set out a blanket and put the blocks on it. They both had brown hair and blue eyes. Tamsin meant twin and she was a robust girl, Brigid meant strong. From what Clarissa was told Brigid almost hadn't made it. She was smaller and shyer than her twin.

Clarissa couldn't help but keep an eye on who was going upstairs. "Dolly?"

Dolly shook her head. "He doesn't want to see you. I'm sure he'll change his mind. Well look at you two girls. You both bring sunshine everywhere you go."

Tamsin smiled first and Brigid copied. Dolly bent and kissed them on the tops of their heads. Then she kissed Clarissa too. "He'll relent soon enough. He's going to be just fine, but boy is he a bear."

Touching her forehead, Clarissa smiled at Dolly. She'd never been kissed on the head before. It felt nice.

SHE STOPPED OVER EVERY DAY, hoping to see Donnell, but he refused to see her. It had only taken her a week of humiliation for her to get the message. It hurt but there was nothing she could do about it. Fitzpatrick teased her and said he'd court her, but she always shook her head and finally she stopped spending time at the main house.

She needed to get a job. Every time she tried to help with the chores around the ranch, she was told it was someone else's job. She did help with the wash since that was done outside the main house. She enjoyed getting to know Dolly.

"Dolly, do you think there might be a few nice men willing to marry? I can't afford to go anywhere else and I'm not sure what the people in town think of me. Do they know I was alone with a man after dark?"

"As far as the town knows you're an upstanding citizen. Most know about what Joe Kingsley did to you and when explained they understood why you rented a room at the saloon. You have your heart set on getting married soon, don't you?"

The back of her throat burned. "I don't feel right being here when Donnell wants me out of his sight. His judgment is rather harsh, and I don't think we'd get on. The only thing I didn't tell him was that my mother worked in the saloon in Bent, and that I was born out of wedlock. I'd only just found out myself. I can't stay here wondering if I'm going to see him or not. I've had too many people leave me behind, including Donnell."

Dolly sighed. " I had such hopes for the two of you. I know Donnell can seem cold at times. He wasn't like that before the war. Come to church with us tomorrow. There's a social after and you can meet more of the town's people."

"I'd like that. I'd like to sit in the house of the Lord. I'm sure it will do me good."

"I'll fix you a basket to sell."

"Why would I want to sell a basket?"

Dolly chuckled. "It's a way to make money for the church. The women bring a basket of food and the men bid on them. Then the winner gets to eat what's in the basket with the one who brought it. It's always fun."

Clarissa put on her brightest smile. "Thank you, it sounds

like fun. The wash is all hung. Do you have anything else that needs doing?"

"No, you go ahead and go home. Enjoy yourself." Dolly turned and walked toward the main house.

Clarissa watched her for a moment and then caught sight of Donnell standing, staring out the window. It looked like he was getting around. No wonder Dolly didn't invite her in for tea. Her shoulders slumped as she walked to her house. There weren't going to be any more invitations to the house. She'd best freshen up her best dress.

CLARISSA WAITED in front of her house, not wanting to be in the way again. She waited until Dolly called her over and she got into the wagon. Then she sat on a bench seat facing the back of the wagon. With so many people going she was surprised she was sitting alone.

Lord, help me to feel worthy of friendship. I always think people won't want to bother with me. What if no one bids on my basket? I want to see the church and participate in the service. I know that it will fill me with happiness. But I'm so nervous about after. I need to remember I am Your child.

It didn't take any time at all before the wagon stopped. Fitzpatrick helped her out, and she gave him a grateful smile. Keeping close to Dolly, she entered the church. She looked at the wooden cross in the front and she felt God.

Many people looked at her, and Dolly nodded her head at each. Clarissa kept a smile on her face, and when Dolly stopped at a pew, she saw Donnell using crutches waiting for the family to move down the pew and have a seat. As Dolly directed the family as to where to sit, she had her arm on Clarissa. Dolly went before her and sat down, leaving Clarissa at the end where she'd be right next to Donnell.

Her stomach churned, and she wanted to run. He looked better than he should, and it pulled at her heart. It got worse when she realized she'd have to share his Bible. She held it so he could steady himself. The pounding of her heart was so loud she hardly heard a word.

At one-point Dolly inched over so Clarissa would have to move closer to Donnell. He shot her an angry glance and immediately jerked away as though she'd burned him. She felt as though she was drowning and couldn't breathe. She moved past Donnell as best as she could without touching him, and with her shoulders back and her head held high, she left the church.

There was a cemetery on the side with a few benches. She sat there apologizing to God. She was just a foolish girl. The sooner she left the Kavanaghs the better. She couldn't take much more. It was as though she was so fragile she'd break. She thought about her mother, longing to forget the ending but remembering all the letters instead. Her father, she couldn't fathom anyone treating a daughter the way he had. She knew she was his, but she refused to acknowledge it out loud. Maybe there was something about her that cried out to others the words *not good enough*.

She could hear the singing from inside and knew they'd be out soon. There was a side door too, and she stood there. She needed to go back in alone and talk to God. She needed to find some kind of strength to get through.

"Oh, there you are!" Dolly said as she stood next to her. "I was concerned when I saw you leave."

"I suddenly felt as though I couldn't breathe so I came outside. I'm quite better now."

"Good." Dolly linked her arm with Clarissa's. "Let's go and get the baskets."

Clarissa smiled for Dolly's sake. She'd gone to much trouble to make her a basket too. They dropped the baskets off at a table and then Dolly walked around introducing Clarissa to the townspeople. It was nice to meet the women. The men seemed to take her measure in a different manner. She wasn't experienced enough to know what they thought.

Donnell had taken a seat on a bench and it looked as though he had plenty of company to keep him entertained. In fact, it seemed the single Kavanagh men were popular with the ladies.

A handsome man with black hair and gray eyes introduced himself. "I'm Ed Calver, I've been looking forward to making your acquaintance. I heard about the predicament Joe Kingsley left you in. Gold fever seems to take over, and a man loses sight of everything else." He smiled.

"It's nice to meet you too."

"I'm just going to come out and tell you my situation," he said with candor. "My wife died about four years ago and left me with three boys to raise. They spend a lot of time with me, but the youngest is just four. My next oldest is six, and the oldest is just about to turn nine. I'd think it a real honor if you'd consider allowing me to court you. You don't need to answer right yet. I'm sure there are plenty of men who will vie for your hand."

"I appreciate your direct approach, Mr. Carver."

"Call me Ed."

She nodded. "I will give your request consideration. I'm flattered."

As soon as he left, she turned to Dolly. "Why isn't he remarried yet?"

"He thought about it once a few years ago, but I think he really loved his wife very much."

Clarissa couldn't help her gaze from landing on Donnell. He never even looked her way. Sighing, she went on and met many single men. Some had children and some didn't. She'd never remember so many names.

A nice-looking man with light brown hair and blue eyes came closer with a bundle in his arms.

"Ma'am, I'm Terry Linch." He moved the blanket revealing the sweetest baby. "This is my boy, Chad. He's six months and his ma, my wife, died in childbirth. I have a good-sized cattle ranch and a nice house. Chad here takes to cow's milk. I got real lucky there. If you don't mind my asking, which basket is yours? I want to be sure to bid on it."

"Her basket has a nest with a red bird in it." Dolly turned to Clarissa. "I put it there after we put them on the table. Sometimes you just want one person to bid."

Clarissa stared at the baby. "May I hold him? I've never held a baby before."

"Ma'am—"

"Call me Clarissa."

"Clarissa, I have a blanket unfolded under that tree." He pointed to one not far from where the bidding would be. "We could sit there and I could show you how."

She glanced at Dolly who gave her a slight nod. "You two go and get acquainted. If you need me, I'll be sitting next to Donnell."

Clarissa's step felt light as she followed Terry to the blanket. He took her hand to help lower her to the ground and then fell to his knees.

"Put your arms like mine. You have to be sure to support the head." He placed Chad in her arms, and she laughed in delight.

"He's tiny. Look, he's grabbing onto my finger."

"He does that."

"I'm sorry for your loss. It must be hard."

He was quiet for a moment. "It's hard taking care of Chad and the ranch. As far as my wife, both our parents pushed us into marriage. We didn't have enough time to know if we'd really get on or not."

Though Clarissa nodded, she wondered what he meant. Did it take a long time to know if you'd get on or not? "He's beautiful. You're blessed to have him."

"I love my little man. I hope you'd give me a chance as far as courting goes. I saw how many men already asked you. Have you made a decision?" He sounded hopeful.

"I'm not entirely sure I'd be good at being a wife and mother. I know nothing about a family and affection seems so foreign to me. I attended an all girls school and I can't remember ever being with my mother. After I graduated, I found out she had died.

"I'm sorry that happened to you. Look, the bidding is about to start."

Another auction came to mind, and she trembled.

"Do you want me to take Chad?"

She nodded and handed Terry the baby. She couldn't help but gaze at Donnell, and this time he stared back at her. She wrapped her arms around her waist. Donnell looked away first, and she felt cold and empty.

"She's suddenly become a social butterfly," Donnell said bitterly.

Dolly put her hand on his arm. "You announced you were just friends. She put her trust in you and quite frankly she's been abandoned at every turn. You were the last in a series of painful leavings."

He sighed. "I didn't think about it that way. All I could see were the lies she told. I couldn't get past them."

Dolly frowned. "Tell me what lie did she tell that was such a betrayal?"

"She never told me what her mother did for a living. She never said why she couldn't go home during school breaks.

She made up some lie about a dress shop. I checked. No one had opened a dress shop in that town. She pretended to be staying at the hotel when she had a room at the saloon. I'm actually surprised there is a Joe Kingsley. Oh, and she conveniently left out the part where the owner of the saloon is her father."

"You have a big list," observed Dolly with a wry smile. "She's as green as they come. The only thing she's guilty of is leading you to believe she was going to stay at the hotel and what her mother did for a living. The whole time she was at school, she really believed there was a dress shop, and finding out what her mother did for a living turned her all around. If you ask me becoming a mail-order bride was her best choice. Except she picked badly." She nodded toward the baskets. "The bidding is starting."

He wasn't in the mood to bid and eat with anyone. Dolly always packed an extra basket that she kept in the wagon.

The auction was boring until one basket was put up. It seemed as though every man wanted it. He recognized that red bird in the nest. It used to be part of someone's ridiculous hat. He frowned as he followed the bidding. Terry Linch sure did want it but had to drop out as the price got over ten dollars.

Donnell saw Hank Thatcher out of the corner of his eye and immediately grabbed his crutch. Hank was bidding. There was no way Hank was going to win only to terrorize Clarissa!

"Twenty," Hank yelled out. He smiled. He probably thought he'd won.

"Thirty," Donnell bid. He scanned the crowd and saw Clarissa's frightened expression. She'd already stood and it looked like she was getting ready to run.

"Thirty-five." Hank sounded confident.

"One hundred," Donnell said firmly.

There was a hush among the crowd. "Going once, going twice, sold to Donnell Kavanagh!"

Donnell smiled, and Hank glared at him.

"Nice leg. I'll get her eventually, you know." A vicious smile curled his lips. "The way I got you."

Donnell felt every one of his brothers stand with him.

"We protect what's ours," Teagan warned.

"Then she belongs to your brother? It's never going to happen." Hank widened his stance. People scurried out of the line of fire.

Donnell took a wobbly step forward and his brother Quinn stopped him. "Listen, mister, I think you should be going."

"Only if my whore comes with me." Hank smiled maliciously.

People immediately started to talk. Donnell heard all the filthy things they said. "She's your daughter. She's no whore. In fact, we're getting married as soon as possible."

"You went ahead and took her, did you? Now she's damaged goods!"

Many of the bystanders gasped.

Donnell's hands fisted. "I won't even dignify that with an answer. All I will say is my bride to be is one of the most honorable women I know."

Dolly smiled at him and nodded.

Sullivan and Brogan each took one of Hank's arms and walked toward the jailhouse.

"What did you mean by telling Donnell you got to him? Shot him, didn't you?" Sullivan spoke loud enough for most to hear.

CHAPTER TEN

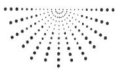

*C*larissa stared down at the sleeping baby. Embarrassment overwhelmed her, and she didn't dare look up. "Give me a moment and I'll leave. Chad is a beautiful boy."

"Are you engaged to Donnell?" Terry asked.

"No, he can't stand me and sometimes it's too uncomfortable at the ranch. It's his family home, that's why I decided to try and find a husband." She finally raised her head and many of the men who had earlier vied for her attention now had their backs to her. Thankfully, she didn't see the anticipated condemnation from most of the women.

She watched as Donnell struggled to get to the table and pick up her basket. He was clumsy with his crutch and the basket but he made it to the blanket where she sat. He gave her a lopsided smile.

"Mind if I join the three of you?"

Terry stood and took the basket, set it on the blanket and helped Donnell to sit on the ground. Clarissa smiled when Terry made sure to position Donnell so he was able to lean back against the tree.

"Clarissa, I'm sorry about the scene I caused."

"It was Hank Thatcher who caused it. I know you were just trying to save me from him." She set the food out and offered Terry the first plateful. Then she made up one for Donnell. "Dolly sure can make fried chicken like no other. It's not that I can't cook because I can, but I didn't know about the social or even what a social was until yesterday. Dolly made up the basket for me."

"That's a fine boy you have, Terry," Donnell commented.

"I'm right proud of him. It's been a hard road, but we're still here together." He gazed at her then at Donnell. "I know you announced your intention to marry Clarissa, but I plan to court her."

She carefully watched Donnell's expression and he looked relieved. "You are welcome to her."

Just like that, he crushed her with his uncaring words. She gave herself a moment before she gazed at Terry. "I would like that." Her face heated, and she pushed her food around her plate. Her appetite had fled.

Chad began to fuss, and she was amazed watching Terry quickly change him and get a bottle out of his saddlebag. "Do you want to feed him?"

She suddenly felt shy but nodded her head. As soon as they were situated, she blocked out everything but the bliss of feeding an infant. The happiness she felt filled her.

"Looks like Chad likes you," Terry commented gently.

"Looks like Clarissa likes the baby," Donnell said with a hint of bitterness in his voice. "You'll make an excellent mother," he said quietly.

Terry put everything back into the basket. Donnell ignored the hint to allow them to be alone. Clarissa wanted to laugh as she watched the two men. Donnell's behavior surprised her. Did he really not want to leave, or was he trying to allow any gossip to die down? She'd never understand him and the best thing for her was to forget him.

"Here let me burp him." Terry lovingly took his son and began patting his back.

"So, this is what you want? A ready-made family with a man you just met?" Donnell scowled at her.

"I don't analyze everything to death the way you do. I probably should, but I'm cautious. Like you said I just met Terry and Chad. He was the first man who didn't look at me and make me feel dull at this church social. He didn't turn away when my father called me a whore or ask me any questions about it. I'd like to get to know him better. Why? Is there something you need to warn me about?"

Donnell struggled to stand, and Terry helped him up. "Thank you for a lovely lunch even if you didn't make it. The company was pleasant. If I don't want to end up in a wagon with all my nieces and nephews I'd best get going." He turned and walked away.

"I'm sorry about that. He doesn't want me he made that very clear but he doesn't want anyone else to have me. So, tell me more about yourself."

THE PAIN of walking was much worse than he let on. He hadn't counted on walking much past the bench he had first sat on. He'd never understand women. He paid a lot of money to get her away from her father and here he was going home without her. He didn't want to be responsible for her yet it must have become such a habit it was hard to quit.

Terry Linch was a nice enough man. It was sad that his wife had died. They'd always looked happy together. His ranch was solid. He had a good business head and wasn't trying to expand too fast. His house looked nice from the outside and he kept the yard around it looking good. He wasn't the one for her though. He couldn't be over his wife. It had only been six or eight months. Clarissa needed lots of love. She had missed out on growing up in a family. He doubted she was even hugged much. Of course, there was the baby boy to hug.

He couldn't believe it was her father who had shot him but it made sense. He was a low-down snake for sure. Donnell admitted he would buy her basket again if it kept her *father* from her. It hurt to see her with another man, but it had to be. He'd never be able to trust her, though Dolly didn't think it was anything to get upset about. In this case Dolly was wrong.

As it turned out he had to wait for a ride home. Apparently, people never left this early. Didn't one of the children need to get home for a nap? He leaned and scowled. Later he turned down the tail gate and sat and scowled.

"You might have to wait a bit. The sack race is taking place," Murphy said as he joined Donnell.

"That's fine." Donnell shrugged his left shoulder.

"When is the wedding?"

"Never. I don't plan to marry, and if I do it will be to someone I can trust. A pretty woman who is innocent. I know there will be some talk, but it'll die down eventually. How do I even know for sure she didn't work at the saloon?" Murphy's eyes widened as he stared at something beyond Donnell, and Donnell turned to see who was behind him, though he had a good guess and he was correct. Clarissa stood there with a world of pain in her eyes. Before he could apologize, she was swiftly walking away.

Clarissa hitched a ride on one of the last wagons. Teagan drove while Gemma and Dolly sat in the front. Clarissa took a fussing Lacey. There wasn't room in the front for all her squirming, but she was happy to sit in Clarissa's lap and sing songs all the way to the ranch.

Teagan pulled up in front of the main house, jumped off the wagon, and then helped Dolly and Gemma down. Next, he took Lacey from Clarissa set her down and finally helped Clarissa.

She gave him a quick smile. "Thank you."

"Sunday supper will be ready in a few hours," Dolly called out.

"I hope you'll excuse me. I'm not feeling up to it."

"If you change your mind you are more than welcome," Dolly told her as she gave her an encouraging smile.

"Thank you." Clarissa turned and walked to her house. She took her bonnet off and gazed at herself in the mirror. There wasn't anything she could do to look pretty. Character should count for something, but Donnell didn't think much of her character anyway. In pain, she quickly turned her back to the mirror.

She took out her Bible and sat in the rocking chair. Dolly had been right introducing Clarissa to everyone. She did need to find a husband, but after her father yelling and then Donnell's announcement of marriage she didn't stand a chance. Everyone knew what a rushed wedding meant. Terry had been nice about it but a man didn't court an engaged woman.

There wouldn't be a wedding. It was devastating that Donnell still thought of her as untrustworthy. She'd kept herself decent and clean for her husband. Somehow, he didn't believe her. There would be no second chance. Donnell could be a hard man at times. Despite it all, she'd kept hope alive that he'd come to care for her. There was no way that was going to happen. All of her dreams had crumbled and how was she supposed to make new ones? Maybe having dreams was stupid.

She'd have to find another man who wants a mail-order bride. Opening her Bible to the Psalms she turned the pages until she came to Psalms 56

A Prayer of Trust

> *Be merciful unto me, O God:*
> *for man would swallow me up;*
> *he fighting daily oppresseth me.*
> *Mine enemies would daily swallow me up:*
> *for they be many that fight against me, O thou Most High.*
> *What time I am afraid,*
> *I will trust in thee.*
> *In God I will praise his word,*
> *in God I have put my trust;*
> *I will not fear what flesh can do unto me.*
> *Every day they wrest my words:*
> *all their thoughts are against me for evil.*
> *They gather themselves together,*
> *they hide themselves,*
> *they mark my steps,*
> *when they wait for my soul.*
> *Shall they escape by iniquity?*
> *In thine anger cast down the people, O God.*
> *Thou tellest my wanderings:*
> *put thou my tears into thy bottle:*
> *are they not in thy book?*
> *When I cry unto thee,*
> *then shall mine enemies turn back:*

this I know; for God is for me.
In God will I praise his word:
in the LORD will I praise his word.
In God have I put my trust:
I will not be afraid what man can do unto me.
Thy vows are upon me, O God:
I will render praises unto thee.
For thou has delivered my soul from death:
Wilt not thou deliver my feet from falling,
That I may walk before God in the light of the living?

HER HEART NEEDED the light and her soul cried out for it.

She heard a buggy stopping. To her dismay it was Reverend Charles, and he was headed her way. He probably wanted to talk about the wedding plans. Taking her handkerchief out she dabbed at her eyes and took a deep breath. When he knocked, she answered.

The reverend took off his hat and nodded in greeting. "I'd like to get to know you a bit before the wedding if that's fine with you."

"Of course, Reverend, please come in. Can I make you coffee?"

"No, I'm actually looking forward to Dolly's coffee." His smile provided a measure of peace.

She led the way into the front room and gestured toward an upholstered chair. She took up her Bible and sat back down in her rocker. "What would you like to know?"

"Truthfully, I'm concerned about the names that man called you and the rush to get married. I understand these things happen, and a quick wedding is ideal."

"Reverend, I have not lain with Donnell."

"Oh, well then…" His face reddened. "If Donnell is stepping up for another man that's a good thing."

"Reverend, I'm pure. The man yelling at the social today is my father. He owns a saloon in Bent, and my mother worked there."

"Oh dear. Did you live there too?" His face grew quite serious.

"They say I was born there, but I don't remember ever being there as a child. I grew up in boarding schools. I graduated recently, and had one envelope my mother wrote her address on. I kept it for years. I went to the town of Bent to find her, and to my dismay the address was Thatcher's Saloon. I thought I had to be wrong. My mother and I made detailed plans about a dress shop and I took extra sewing classes. But I found mother was dead and there was never a store."

"How is it you're here?"

"I foolishly decided to become a mail-order bride. Joe Kingsley was supposed to be my groom, but rumor has it he took one look and decided I wasn't pretty enough. I met Donnell and he took me here to meet Dolly. He thinks everything I've told him is a lie and he doesn't trust me, and I will not marry a man who can't look me in the eye." She clasped her hands and laid them on her Bible.

"My father decided to come fetch me and make me work off my mother's contract. He also put me up for auction in his saloon." Her face grew increasingly heated. "Fortunately, Donnell rescued me and proved the contract invalid. I was bowled over today when Donnell announced our intent to marry. He never even asked me." She sighed, and her shoulders dropped.

"Donnell was trying to protect you I imagine."

"Yes Reverend, he was, and I foolishly thought that maybe, just maybe he'd come to like me, but I walked up to Murphy and Donnell, and Donnell said a few things about me. He doesn't want to marry me and after he said such uncomplimentary things, I don't want to marry him either."

"I'm so sorry, Clarissa. I was looking forward to the wedding ceremony, but both the man and woman must be willing. I wish there was something I could do for you."

"I'm going to be just fine. I have my faith and that will see me through."

"There are many Kavanaghs who are still single."

She shook her head. "I'm going to go elsewhere. I can't look at Donnell day after day."

"You need to forgive him, Clarissa."

"It's not that, Reverend. I care for him too much to see him eventually marry another woman."

His brows lifted. "I understand. Can I escort you to Sunday supper?"

"No. I don't want to talk about why we aren't getting married. You enjoy Dolly's cooking." She smiled at him as she stood. She led the reverend to the door. "Thank you for stopping by."

"Bless you." He touched her hand lightly before he left.

DONNELL WAS ACUTELY aware Clarissa wasn't at the supper table. His brothers kept shooting him questioning looks, but he shrugged his shoulders. He'd hurt her but, heck, he didn't even know why he said such things. Hurt pride and his ego had also taken a beating.

"Who is going to make the announcement that the wedding is off?" Reverend Charles asked.

Donnell could barely breathe with the big lump that formed in his throat. He swallowed hard. "I will have to do it."

"Poor Clarissa, this hasn't helped her reputation one bit.

You do know what a soon as possible wedding implies don't you?" Dolly gave him a hard stare.

"I just didn't want her father to buy her basket. I wasn't thinking about how it would look to others. I said we would be married the soonest possible to make him stop yelling such vile words at Clarissa. I'm sure if I explain it to the right people, they will let everyone else in the town know there was no real reason for a hurried wedding. Besides we do not suit. In fact, I don't think she even likes me."

Murphy cocked his head. "Are you sure about that last part? I see the way she looks at you and it looks to me she is smitten with you."

Donnell glanced around the table and sighed when he saw everyone nodded in agreement. "Reverend Charles, I'm sorry you've been misled, and I take full responsibility for it. We'll figure something out for Clarissa. She's welcome to stay here as long as she needs."

Donnell listened to the murmurs and knew he was outgunned. He took his cup of coffee and went outside to the back porch so as not to be disturbed. He looked up at the sky, admiring the bright stars. He felt awful even though he explained he'd done the damage to Clarissa's reputation to save her. He could marry her, but it would never be a happy marriage. Heck, he couldn't even trust her to tell the truth. He took a long deep sip of his coffee. When had he become so rigid? When had he started to think in black and white only? Most of the things in the world are shades of gray. It was quiet except for the leaves in the trees as a warm breeze blew. Maybe it was fear that kept him from caring for any other woman. He kept thinking about what happened to his mother. His father had been very cold and callous and what he'd done he hadn't done alone. It had involved another woman. He didn't blame his mother for being bitter any longer. It still hurt, it felt as though she'd taken her love for him away. One day she'd give hugs and kisses and the next day nothing. That was what lies led to, bitter nothing. He also remembered his parents had stopped speaking to each other around that time. He didn't want to take a chance that would happen to him. Yep, it was fear that was holding him back, but he didn't know how to let go.

Lord me help with this, I'd sure appreciate it. Clarissa is a nice girl, and she doesn't deserve everything that has been dumped on her. I'm afraid I'm the cause of a lot of it. I don't know what happened. I thought I cared for her, and I thought she was beginning to care for me. Help me to do right by her. Please Lord, I don't want to hurt her again.

A shooting star crossed the sky, and he wondered if it was a sign of renewed hope. He stood and rubbed his hand over his face. There was nothing else he could do tonight, he might as well try to get some shut eye.

CHAPTER ELEVEN

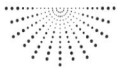

It had been more than a week since the Sunday social. Clarissa still didn't have a plan, and she grew more anxious by the day. Everyone had been so nice and reassuring that she could stay but she really needed to go. First, she needed to go to town and find a newspaper. Hopefully there would be a few ads for mail-order brides. She'd been avoiding going into town, she didn't want to answer any questions about Hank Thatcher. She wasn't even sure he was still in jail; no one had told her one way or the other.

It was her own fault; she'd kept to herself most of the week. She did help Dolly with the wash, and she weeded the plant beds. Dolly kept inviting her over for supper, but she always declined. The less she saw of Donnell the better. She didn't want to set brother against brother; it just wouldn't be right.

She glanced out the front window and saw a wagon in front of the main house. Quickly, she grabbed her shawl and bonnet and headed over to the main house.

"You're welcome to come along," Dolly offered cheerfully.

Clarissa smiled. "I'd be delighted to go with you. I have some business I need to take care of."

"Why don't you sit in the middle and I'll sit beside you," Dolly suggested. She extended her hand out to Clarissa and helped her up on to the wagon. Then Dolly scrambled up and sat next to her. "I have kind of a long list, but I'm hoping it won't take too terribly long."

Heat washed over Clarissa's face as Dolly stared at her. "I thought I'd see if I could find any ads for mail-order brides. After all, that's why I'm here. You just never know… I might find the right one this time."

"What about your dress shop? I thought that had been your dream since you were a small girl."

"I've come to realize that sometimes you have to let go of your old dreams and make new ones. I'll never be able to afford a dress shop. I'm just being practical about it. But I would like to have a husband and children. I think a big family would suit me." Clarissa's face was on fire as the wagon was jostled. Donnell was climbing aboard; apparently he was going to be the driver, and he'd probably heard most of her conversation.

"Hello Donnell, how have you been?"

He gave her a quick glance before he grabbed the reins. "Just fine I'm doing just fine. And you? I haven't seen much of you this past week. You even missed Sunday services."

"I'm sure God knows where I was. He knows what's in my heart and that's all it matters. Plus, I didn't want to hear all the women gossiping, wondering when the wedding is going to be." She stared straight ahead as the wagon began to move.

"You don't have to worry about that anymore. I announced the end of our wedding plans. I didn't give a reason. I figured if you wanted to that would be fine."

Clarissa turned toward Dolly. "What was the reaction of the congregation?"

Dolly hesitated for a moment. She put her hand on Clarissa's arm. "There was the usual speculation but the rumors of you being with child were squashed. I'm just so sorry about how all this came about. You don't have to tell anybody anything. It's not their business."

Clarissa nodded as relief surged through her. Hopefully the trip to town wouldn't be as painful as she thought it might be.

"Is there something you need in town, Clarissa?" asked Donnell.

"I thought I'd try to find a few mail-order bride ads. I can't just stay in that house; I need to move ahead. Plus, I want to know what is happening with Hank Thatcher. I haven't heard a word."

"They just let him go. There wasn't any proof that he shot me. But everyone knows he did. As long as he never comes to this town again I don't much care." He tightened his hands on the reins. "I still think we need to be on guard though. He's not the type to go quietly."

"I'm sorry, Donnell. You getting shot is all my fault. You probably wish I never came to Texas at all. But don't you worry, I plan to move on as soon as I can."

Donnell didn't say a word; he just looked very tense. He didn't want to talk to her, she knew it. She wished it was otherwise, but she didn't know what to do or what to say. Leaving would be the best thing for them both. It was a relief when they finally got to town.

Donnell easily got off the wagon and immediately helped Dolly down to the planked walk. Before Clarissa had a chance to get herself down Donnell had his hands around her waist. There was something about him and she felt it every time he was near. It was worse if they happened to touch but she didn't know what it was. She only knew it had to be special. He set her down, but his hands lingered at her waist as he gazed at her. She stared at his vest. It wasn't until she met his gaze that he let go and took a step back.

She hurried into the store with Dolly on her heels. Space was what she needed and time away from Donnell's penetrating stare. Dolly stopped to look at some new kitchen wares as Clarissa walked all the way to the back counter.

"Good day, Miss. Plunkett," John O'Rourke greeted. "How can I help?"

Clarissa quickly looked around to make sure no one could hear her. "I was wondering if you had any ads for mail-order brides." She clasped her hands in front of her feeling like a fool.

John turned around to the big counter behind him and grabbed what looked to be a booklet. He turned back toward her and smiled. "Mail-order brides have gotten to be so plentiful that this here booklet has ads for both men and women. Can you imagine that?"

She took the offered paper and smiled. "How much do I owe you for this?"

"Considering what you've been through with your last mail-order adventure you can have it for free. I hope you find someone in there. I was sad to hear that the wedding was called off. I thought you and Donnell made a handsome couple. Was there anything else I can get for you?"

She had started looking through the pages and became flustered when Donnell's name came up. "No, no that will be all and thank you so much." She turned and hurried out the door.

Donnell walked around town trying to think of something to do to kill time. He didn't know the new sheriff well enough to stop in and chew the fat. The barbershop was too crowded, and he wasn't hungry. He tipped his hat at every female he came across. He especially liked to see the older women smile back at him. So, she was looking for a new groom. It should have made him happy it should have made him feel relieved, but it didn't.

He couldn't imagine himself married to Clarissa, yet he didn't want to let her go. Not that she'd ever let him have a say as to whether she left or not. He smiled. She wasn't as shy now as she had been when she first came here. It must be hard not having a home or family. No matter what, he always knew that Dolly and his brothers were there for him. It was a comforting feeling. He leaned against a post across the road from where Clarissa sat. He wasn't sure why he'd ever thought her to be unattractive. Her blond hair looked silky, and idly he wondered how long it was. When she smiled which wasn't often around him her blue eyes sparkled. He watched her read and he could see a little furrow in her brow as she concentrated. Why would she still think being a mail-order bride a good idea? He shook his head.

The noise got louder down at the saloon and a few men barreled out. Early drinkers. He shook his head. He saw their interest narrow in on Clarissa. There was going to be trouble, he could feel it.

He crossed the road and got to her side about the same time as the other three men. She looked confused as though she didn't realize the danger she could be in with these drunkards.

"Clarissa, may I help you into the wagon?"

She seemed relieved as she took the hand he offered.

"You wouldn't be that Plunkett gal, would you?" The man

asking looked as though he hadn't washed his face or combed his hair in weeks.

Clarissa met Donnell's gaze. She didn't seem to know what to do. She stood and held on to his hand.

"Who might you be?" Donnell asked in a no-nonsense voice.

The man smiled showing the few teeth he had left. "She's my fiancé. I do believe I paid to have her come out here to Texas. That gives me first claim on her."

Clarissa put her hand over her mouth as her eyes grew wider. "Joe Kingsley?"

"Yeah that's me. You know where the preacher is? We should get ourselves hitched while we're in town. I wouldn't want anyone to steal you from me." He chuckled but lay his hand on the butt of his gun.

Clarissa had quite a grip. She had both hands squeezing his one hand. Donnell positioned himself so that he stood in front of Clarissa. "I think you lost your claim to this woman when you left her without funds or a place to live. She's been here for quite a long time. I'd be willing to pay you back for your expenses in getting her here, but that's it."

Joe glanced from one friend to the other and shook his head. "I guess you don't know who you're talking to. So I'll let what you just said go. Men know to respect me now. Haven't you heard I struck it rich? I bet I'm richer than all you Kavanaghs. If I'm saying I want that woman I want that woman and not you or anybody else is going to take her from me."

The man standing on Kingsley's right side lunged toward Clarissa. She screamed loudly. Donnell blocked the man until he backed off. But when Donnell turned back toward Kingsley, he found a gun in his face. Donnell didn't move; he just stared.

"Whoa! Whoa folks what's going on here?" The sheriff asked. "Put that gun down."

Kingsley put his gun back into its holster. But he didn't step back.

The sheriff put himself between Donnell and Kingsley. "Let's work this out peacefully. Now somebody tell me what's going on."

"That there gal is my mail-order bride. I sent her a lot of money to get her here and I'm getting the feeling she ain't gonna marry me. But she's bought and paid for and she's mine."

The sheriff stared at Clarissa for a moment. "Weren't you the one involved with Hank Thatcher?" He turned to Kingsley. "Did you buy her from Hank Thatcher?"

"Hank Thatcher is my father. Though I just met him a few weeks ago. He didn't sell me to anyone. He has no right. I came to Texas as Mr. Kingsley's mail-order bride but he never came to collect me. I waited and waited without any money and wondered what I was supposed to do. I had just enough money to rent a room for one night above the saloon. I've never been so hungry in my life. I was very frightened and didn't know what to do. When I asked around no one had heard of Joe Kingsley. It was odd, very odd. Donnell Kavanagh was gracious enough to bring me out to his ranch and give me a place to stay. I stayed in a house by myself so there was no impropriety at all. In fact, Donnell tried to track down Mr. Kingsley. He discovered Mr. Kingsley was mining for gold and decided that gold was better than a mail-order bride. It also came to my attention Mr. Kingsley was indeed in town when I arrived. He took one look at me and said I was not good enough. I wasn't pretty enough for him. I would say he's the lowest of low."

"Is this true?" The sheriff asked Kingsley.

"Well it ain't a lie. She never found herself another fella so our engagement stands. I done told you she's mine."

The bells above the door of the general store rang. Dolly stepped out with both hands on her hips. She gave Kingsley her best glare. "Well that's where you're wrong. Donnell is going to marry Clarissa. He told everybody two weeks ago. We talked to the Reverend and all there is left to do is for the two of them to pick a date. So, Mr. Kingsley your claim is not valid. I want you to stay away from Clarissa."

Donnell's heart skipped a beat as his stomach dropped. Leave it to Dolly to marry him off any way she could. He took a deep breath but realized Dolly was only protecting Clarissa. "Why that's why Clarissa is here today in town that is, she wanted to get a few things for her wedding dress." He turned to put his arm around Clarissa's shoulders and gave her a squeeze. "Isn't that right, honey?"

Donnell felt her stiffen. "Of course, sugar pie."

Kingsley narrowed his eyes and glared. "I don't believe you for one red-hot minute. I think the best thing to do is for me and Clarissa to get hitched right now."

Donnell wasn't sure what to say. Somehow, he needed to outmaneuver Kingsley. He swallowed hard and looked into Clarissa's eyes. "I agree. Let's get the Reverend so Clarissa and I can get married right now."

HER BODY TREMBLED as she tried to decide what to do. For someone who didn't approve of lies they certainly did fall easily from Donnell's tongue. She stepped away from him so she could look him in the eye. If she saw something anything that would lead her to believe that he cared for her she would go along with his lie. She looked and looked and at first, he just returned her stare. Her back was against the wall and if she didn't say yes Kingsley might just have a claim. Then she saw a flicker in Donnell's blue eyes. If she was wrong, it would be the biggest mistake she ever made. But was this so different from being a mail-order bride again? Did Donnell realize how much he was giving up by marrying her? She would never be enough for him, and she certainly wasn't pretty, that much she was positive of. His eyes grew softer, and she nodded her head.

"Yes, Donnell let's do it now. I don't want anything to ruin our happiness, and I certainly don't want Mr. Kingsley's proposal hanging over my head."

Her heart warmed as Donnell kissed her on the cheek.

"I'll go get the reverend," he said.

John O'Rourke laughed. "I think Dolly beat you to it."

Kingsley swore and spit on the ground. "I won't forget this Kavanagh. Clarissa we could've been good together." She watched as all three men turned and made their way back into the saloon.

Dolly hustled down the street with the reverend in tow. She was out of breath, but she was smiling. "I get to be maid of honor!" She made sure everyone stood in the proper places before she stood next to Clarissa. "It's a wonderful day for an outdoor wedding."

CHAPTER TWELVE

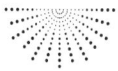

Clarissa stood by the door to the house she'd been living in and watched as Donnell brought his things inside. He'd been almost silent since the wedding that morning. She grew more anxious with each breath. How was she supposed to act? Welcoming? Happy? Excited? Anxiety filled her and nothing else. At least with a mail-order arrangement the groom wanted to get married- with the exception of Joe.

Donnell did not look like a happy husband. He could be so stubborn. He might never care for her. A house with no smiles was what she imagined.

"I need to get to work." He walked out the door.

Her heart plummeted. She knew but she'd hoped he'd show some type of affection. He barely kissed her at the wedding. He kept his body from touching hers the whole ride home, and when he lifted her down from the wagon, he acted as though she was as hot as coals. He let go of her so fast she almost stumbled. Then he murmured something about getting his things and left.

Dolly smiled and hugged her. It had been so hard to keep

a smile on her face, but she did for Dolly's sake. Then Clarissa quickly turned and left.

The wish that he'd act differently when he moved in wasn't granted. If she had a choice, she would have chosen Donnell but only if he'd chosen her too. She'd taken his freedom away from him and he'd probably never forgive her. Standing alone in the house she yearned for his arms around her. He could have stayed for just a minute or two. Now everyone will know he was forced to marry her.

And what about the children she wanted to have? The rest of the wives had been blessed and Gemma would have her baby in about four or five months. A child gave unconditional love didn't it? Just once she wanted to know what it felt like.

Sighing she grabbed two sets of clean sheets and made up the bigger bed that she'd been sleeping in for Donnell. She made up the smaller one in the other room for herself. Then she moved her things into the smaller room. She'd let Donnell put his things where he wanted. Now what should she make for supper? It would be their first meal as husband and wife. Surely something special was called for.

She had venison Sullivan had shared with her, and thankfully she'd picked vegetables the day before. She couldn't face anyone today. She couldn't possibly have the happy glow a bride usually had. Maybe if she thanked him for his sacrifice it would make a difference. Yes, she would thank him and smile and act happy. That was bound to change things.

She got busy making stew and she also made cornbread to go with it. Soon the coffee was on the stove. Quickly she went and put on a pretty dress and took her time putting her hair up so it looked nice. The sound of the door opening set her heart pounding. She moistened her lips and went to greet him.

"Hello—"

Donnell frowned and interrupted her. "Get ready. We're eating at the main house."

She just stood and stared.

"Go on and fix yourself up while I wash." He poured water into a basin and took it into his room.

Clarissa didn't move. There wasn't anything more she could do to make herself presentable. Her shoulders slumped but she refused to cry. Instead she took everything off the stove. Her food wouldn't be needed.

Dolly probably wanted to do something special for them. If only she'd sent word before all the food was prepared. She grabbed her wrap and stood near the door.

Donnell hurried out of the bedroom and ushered her out the front door. Before he closed the door, he frowned at her.

Donnell's stride was long, and she had to practically run to keep up with him. She never put on her wrap. She'd seen Teagan and Quinn putting them on their wives. Maybe it would take Donnell a while to get used to married life.

Dolly opened the door before they even climbed the steps to the porch. She hugged Donnell and let go. Her smile dimmed a bit. Her gaze searched Clarissa's before she hugged her extra hard.

"Everyone is here. We fed the children first, and Orla volunteered to watch then while we have a celebration supper."

"That sounds wonderful, Dolly. Thank you for going to so much trouble for Donnell and me." At his sharp look, she realized he didn't want her to speak for him. He'd been a good man. What happened to her friend?

She was hugged by Ciara, Heaven, Sheila and then Gemma. "What a blessing it is to have you in our family," Gemma enthused.

Everyone was seated, and it hurt to see the affection between the brothers and their wives. That was what she wanted, and her determination to have it grew. She listened while they all had stories to tell about their children. When she dared to glance at Donnell out of the corner of her eye, she could see his frown. Frankly, she was tired of seeing it, but she'd have to put up with it.

"You should have seen Donnell rescue me from Joe Kingsley!" Clarissa tried her best to sound excited.

Everyone wanted to know the story, and for the rest of the meal Donnell was at the center of attention. At least he wasn't frowning and that was a good thing. Maybe he was just in a mood and everything would be fine. But she couldn't help the doubt that crept into her mind.

At the end Dolly came out with a beautiful cake for their wedding. The icing was pure white, and Clarissa's cheeks bloomed with warmth as she realized the meaning of the white icing. It was a symbol of the bride's virginity.

"It is so beautiful, Dolly, thank you so very much for making this day special for us."

Dolly put the cake in front of Clarissa and handed her a knife. Clarissa stood ready to cut the cake when Dolly made Donnell stand up too. "If you both cut the first piece of cake it's good luck."

Clarissa took the knife and gave it to Donnell. He held the knife and waited for her to put her hand on his and then he cut the first slice. He glanced at Clarissa and smiled. "It sure looks good. Thank you Dolly."

Dolly beamed as she sliced the rest of the cake and handed it out to each. She went into the kitchen and grabbed the coffee pot then returned and poured everyone a cup.

Sullivan lifted his cup. "To much love, laughter, and children. That's my wish for you." Everyone lifted their cup and toasted to the couple.

DONNELL WASN'T sure how much longer he could pretend to be happy. Just because they got married that morning everyone expected instant happiness from him. He didn't work that way. Maybe one day he'd be able to look at Clarissa with love in his eyes, but he didn't know when that would be. He felt things for her, but he wasn't sure what it all meant. If she had really wanted to marry him, she wouldn't have asked for the ads to be a mail-order bride.

Clarissa had icing at the top of her lip, and Donnell had the sudden urge to kiss her. He quickly turned from her. There would be no urges until he decided there would be. He glanced at her again and took his napkin gently wiping away the icing. It was going to be a fine line trying not to look like an idiot to his wife in public.

He was grateful that she understood. He noticed how she moved her things from the bigger bedroom. She was understanding, and he was happy he wouldn't have a weeping woman on his hands.

It started getting late, and everyone needed to go and collect their children. It was always a long goodbye with his family. There were so many hands to shake and always a lot of hugs. It was a relief when he and Clarissa left the house. He noticed as they walked across the yard that she didn't put her wrap around her shoulders. Right, because husbands usually did that for their wives. He'd have to observe and make a list of what he was supposed to do.

He opened the door and gestured for her to go in first. Clarissa sat in her rocking chair while he took a seat across from her. "What a day. I know when I woke up this morning, I wasn't planning on getting married."

She stiffened and lowered her gaze to her lap. "I know you didn't, and I can't tell you how sorry I am. I know this isn't what you want and if there had been any other way, I would've taken it. You're a good man, Donnell, and I'm sorry that you didn't get to choose the wife of your dreams. I can cook, clean, do the wash, and stay out of your way. Actually, if you'd rather I can eat before you come home. So I agree, what a day."

Donnell didn't know what to say. He hadn't looked at any of this from her perspective. Now he wasn't sure how to act around her and that was unlike him. How did he show friendship and compassion without her getting the wrong idea? "I think it might take a bit of practice but we can share the house and give each other space. My routine is pretty much the same day in and day out, working the ranch. I think if we get that figured out we'll be just fine."

She glanced up at him again, but this time he didn't see anger on her face or in her eyes. Good, she was willing to make the best of it. It didn't matter really. At least he already knew her background and all of her secrets. It was much easier than trying to find another woman to be his wife.

"Is there anything you need before I head into bed?"

"No, you go right ahead. I want to tidy up the kitchen and read my Bible before I go to bed. Donnell… thank you again for rescuing me. I know this isn't what you wanted but I appreciate it so much."

He nodded and lit another lamp to take into the bedroom with him. He didn't say another word; he just went inside sat on his bed and wondered how it had all happened. He shook his head. Hadn't he just promised himself he wasn't going to look at the world in black-and-white anymore, that he was going to try to see the shades of gray? He had to admit she looked pretty in her dress tonight but he didn't feel comfortable telling her so. He will have to try to do better. There was no sense living the rest of their lives in misery.

THE NEXT DAY Clarissa marveled at the way Donnell gave her real smiles. Perhaps there was hope for them after all. She'd have to be patient, but last night as she lay in bed she realized she loved that ornery man more than she had thought.

Her heart was lighter when he headed to work. She looked around the house with a critical eye, trying to decide if she needed to change anything. She hadn't looked at it that way before because she never planned to stay long. Curtains. She could definitely use new curtains. All she needed was the material and some sewing supplies. It wouldn't cost very much at all.

She forgot to ask him if he was going to come in for the noon meal. She had bread baking in the oven, so she could make him a sandwich or something and hope it was good enough. Now what did he say about giving each other space? He was right his routine was pretty much the same every day. All she needed to do was to figure out her routine so they wouldn't keep bumping into each other.

How do other brides feel when they first get married? She'd expected that marriage with Joe Kingsley would be awkward since she didn't know him. But what about marriages where the people knew each other? Did they experience awkwardness too? She wasn't about to ask anyone. It would only embarrass Donnell. For now, she would have to keep her own counsel.

Noontime came and went without Donnell making an appearance. It made her both upset and relieved at the same time. She'd have to add respect to the list of things they needed to work out. She could go visit Dolly and Gemma but she knew she wouldn't be good company. The whole house was clean so she sat in her rocker and read her Bible.

Later in the afternoon she put the stew back on the stove to heat. She put the coffee on to boil, but she waited before she put the cornbread back into the oven to heat. The days were beginning to grow longer and she waited and waited, but there was no sign of Donnell. She ate supper without him. Maybe he was trying to pretend she didn't exist.

All this worrying was exhausting. She left a lamp on for her missing husband and then took one into her room. She changed into her nightgown, slipped into bed and fell asleep.

Donnell waited outside until he knew that Clarissa had gone to bed. The light in her room had just turned off. He was a coward. He wished he knew more about women. He'd had a long time to think out on the range, and he'd come to the conclusion that he would court his wife. Now all he had to do was figure out how to do that.

CHAPTER THIRTEEN

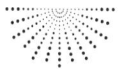

Donnell woke the next morning surprised the house was so quiet. He dressed and then walked into the kitchen. Clarissa must still be sleeping. He could just go to the bunkhouse and grab some coffee. Maybe he could grab some flowers on the way back. All women loved flowers.

He was heartily congratulated by the men in the bunkhouse and that actually made him feel good. He carried his coffee while he looked for flowers. There were some growing right in front of their house, how convenient. He picked a few of the pink ones and a few of the red. He carried them all in one hand and went back into the house.

The smell of bacon and the sound of it sizzling made him hungry. He was hoping for some of the bread she had made yesterday. He'd sampled it last night, and it was good. He put the coffee cup on the table and then he went and stood next to Clarissa.

She glanced at him and turned away. "I'm sorry I overslept. From now on I'll have your breakfast ready so you can eat in silence. It's almost done."

"Don't worry about it. I know you are tired. Everyone deserves to sleep in every now and then." She turned and gave him a surprised look. He handed her the flowers and instead of looking delighted she looked very puzzled.

"These are for me?"

He nodded

"I've never had flowers before. Thank you." Her hands trembled as she took them from him.

He watched as she put them into a large glass and added water. She bent over a few times to smell them. It had been worth the effort to pick a few flowers to see such a bright smile on her face.

"Can I ask you something?" Clarissa asked.

"Sure, go ahead."

"What do these flowers mean exactly?" She almost looked as though she was going to cry.

"I saw them and thought my wife might like to have some. I also realized what a numbskull I've been. I'm acting as though I don't want you, and that couldn't be further from the truth. There was something about you that intrigued me the first time I saw you. The feeling grew, and it scared me." A sheepish smile formed on his lips. "I also realized you are right. You never did lie to me but I was trying to find a reason to distance myself from you. I never thought you'd stay this long, and quite frankly I wanted to be the one who left the relationship — what there was of one — first. I know not all women leave. Look at Dolly. She's been here for us through thick and thin. I should've thought about her and what an example *she* set instead of my mother. I somehow got it into my head that you would love me one day and walk away the next. I had a long time to think yesterday, and I realized what a fool I've been. I should've married you weeks ago, but I wasn't sure how you felt. What I'm really trying to say is, Clarissa will you be my wife and the mother of my children?"

Clarissa walked away and sat at the table. A gamut of expressions played across her face.

Now he was nervous. Him and his idiotic rule of giving each other space is coming back to haunt him. He needed to convince her, and he needed to do it fast. He kneeled in front of her and took both her hands in his and waited until she met his gaze. "I'm hoping you can forgive me. I think we could be happy together. I love you, Clarissa, and I have for quite some time. It scared me how much I love you. I'm hoping you'll forgive me."

Clarissa nodded as tears flowed down her face. "You're right, you have been a numbskull, but you're *my* numbskull. I love you too. I felt so unlovable for so long that I figured that's how you felt about me. I know I'm not pretty, and I wish I was, but I am what I am."

Donnell took all the food off the stove and then went back to Clarissa. "I'm ashamed that I said that, particularly because I don't mean it. When you look at me with your eyes shining with happiness there is nothing more beautiful in the whole wide world." He pulled her into his arms and held her, rocking her back and forth as she cried.

She looked up at him and sniffled. "Does this mean you want children with me?"

"I'd love for us to have a big family. I'll take whatever God gives us."

EPILOGUE

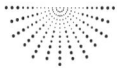

*F*ive months later

CLARISSA SMILED as she watched her husband walking toward the house. Donnell had made it a habit to stop there for his noon meal. They'd had many awkward moments, but now Clarissa felt loved. Donnell touched her every time he walked by, whether it was squeezing her hand, a touch on her shoulder or a kiss on her cheek. It's what she always wanted, but it took her a while to get used to it. Now she wouldn't have it any other way. She loved her affectionate husband.

She looked around at the many trunks and crates scattered through the house. Donnell had built her a brand-new house and they were almost set to move. They would have many happy times in the new place. She'd been keeping an eye on the main house; Ciara was due anytime now.

Sheila was on hand to help, but Clarissa never having a child wouldn't be much help. She imagined she'd only be in the way. She couldn't wait for the baby to be born. Every night when she and Donnell sat in their chairs, she sewed. Ciara and Brogan's baby would be beautifully outfitted.

She hoped and hoped as she sewed that the need for her to sew her own baby clothes would come, but she hadn't been blessed in that way. She sighed as she continued to pack. The Lord did things in his time but she couldn't help but be impatient. The disappointment made her feel guilty since Donnell wanted a big family.

The last two months it had been hard to be around Ciara and Gemma. They both glowed and were happy as can be. She turned when the door opened and put a cheerful smile on her face for her husband.

"Let me get you some cool water. It must be hotter than Hades working out there."

Donnell smiled and his eyes twinkled. "Ciara's baby is on its way. You will be an aunt again. I can't wait to see Ciara's eyes when she sees the wonderful clothes you made. And I'll be standing proudly next to you."

"The baby is coming? I've been watching out the window all day and I hadn't seen any action. It's just as well, I'm not needed." Clarissa put the plate full of sandwiches on the table, and then she got some cool water for them both. She was surprised Donnell hadn't already sat down.

She yelped in surprise as Donnell picked her up and swung her around. He finally set her down and cupped her cheeks in his hands.

"You are always needed. I don't want you to think otherwise. The reason they don't have you over there is because women who haven't had a child might be frightened by the screams. It has nothing to do with how they feel about you. They all love you almost as much as I do." He smiled. "I know it's hard to get used to having so many people around all the time."

He made her feel treasured, and it was a feeling she'd never thought to wish for. "You're right, but sometimes I can't help thinking the way I used to. I think I'm making progress, though. Just look at us, we laugh and we talk and hold each other and truthfully I wasn't sure we'd ever get there. Plus you make me feel safe."

He wrapped his arms around her. "Protecting you hasn't been much of a job. It still amazes me and bewilders me that Hank Thatcher died in the saloon fire. I also find it very interesting that everyone but him escaped. However it happened, it's been a great relief to both of us. I'm hungry."

They ate their sandwiches and she tried to think of something to say but all she could think about was being incapable of giving him the one thing he wanted most a child. They never talked about it, she just knew.

"Out with it. I can see something else is bothering you and you might as well tell me because you know I'll find out anyway."

She put her hands in her lap and stared at them. How did one talk about their failings? She looked up at him and met his gaze. His eyes were full of love and compassion. How could she not tell him how she felt? He was right, it was tell him now or tell him later.

"It's hard to talk about, I think about it every morning and every night and many times during the day. I failed you by my inadequacies. You should've gone with your gut instinct and not married me, I'm sure you'd be much happier with a different wife." Donnell started to stand up. "No, sit down, please. It's just that we both want children and I long for a family. I wait and wait, but God never blesses me with a child. It's been five months we might as well face the fact I'm barren. It shames me, but it shouldn't surprise me. Nothing goes as planned for me anyway."

"I guess telling you to relax won't be of any help. Do I

want children? Yes, I do, but we can only have what we are blessed with. Truthfully, right now I feel like the luckiest man on earth because I have you. Whether or not you give me a child won't change the way I feel. I tried and tried to push away my feelings for you, and I almost pushed too hard. I wasn't sure even after we were married that we'd make our way to a loving marriage. Personally, I'm thankful for Joe Kingsley and I'm definitely thankful that he sent for you. As far as family, we have many members. You have to agree, sometimes we have too many. Everyone seems to have their own opinion, but we work it out at the end. If there was a way for me to put a child in your arms, I would do it. I only know one way and I think we've been doing our part. The rest is out of our hands. So you have no shame, you have no guilt, and you need not worry. I will always and I mean always be here for you. You fill my heart, make me smile, and you show me all the gray areas in life. I feel calmer and I'm much happier not having to feel like I must have the answer to everything. You've done that for me."

Tears filled her eyes and poured down her face. She quickly got her handkerchief and mopped up her tears. They'd be going to the main house soon, and she didn't want anyone feeling sorry for her. Donnell was right, she didn't need to dwell on the things she wanted, she needed to count her blessings for the things she had.

"Feeling better?" Donnell reached across the table and took her hand in his.

"You've certainly opened my eyes. We have our entire lives in front of us and that is a blessing. It's hard to watch the other women have children but you're right, there is no shame and there shouldn't be any guilt about something I can't control." She took a couple deep breaths and she could feel her heart expanding. Glancing out the window, her eyes widened. "I think the baby has been born."

Donnell stood still holding her hand as he walked toward her. "Are you sure you want to go over now? We could wait till later if you wish."

She walked into his arms and hugged him to her. "Let's go see our newest family member."

DONNELL CARRIED the big basket full of the clothes Clarissa had so lovingly sewn. It was good to see her smiling. He wished he had known she was suffering, but she hid it well. He'd been so busy with the ranch and building a new house, he'd had little time to think about it. He learned a long time ago that everything happened in God's time. He used to hate it when people said that to him. It was as though they didn't have an answer. But he was learning he couldn't absolutely have control over everything. All he needed was Faith.

"I'm proud of you. I love you so much, Clarissa." They were at the door to the main house before she had a chance to answer.

As soon as they stepped foot into the house, he could feel the excitement and happiness of his family, their family. Clarissa smiled at everyone and hugged all the women.

"Boy or girl?" she asked.

Dolly beamed. "He's a beautiful, beautiful baby. They named him Benjamin. You can go on up and take a peek if you like."

Donnell took Clarissa's hand and led her up the stairs. Brogan looked out the door and smiled.

"Congratulations!" Clarissa said.

"Go on in. Ciara is still awake."

CLARISSA TIPTOED in and smiled at the beautiful picture Ciara and Benjamin made. It was lovely.

Ciara opened her eyes. "Come Clarissa meet your nephew Benjamin."

Clarissa hurried over to the side of the bed so she could look down on Benjamin's face. "Why he's just an angel, a beautiful angel. I just wanted to drop off a few things I made for you and then I'll let you get back to resting."

Donnell handed Clarissa the basket and stood next to her as she picked up a bundle of clothes.

Ciara looked over each piece with tears in her eyes. "I've never seen anything as beautiful as these clothes. You are truly talented." Her eyes drooped and Clarissa put the clothes back in the basket and set the basket on the dresser.

Brogan thanked them as he sat on the bed next to his wife and son.

Clarissa took a big breath and was glad when Donnell gave her hand a quick squeeze. She heard all the laughter and fun down on the main floor and for a moment felt a bit of jealousy. She'd have to work on not being disappointed. Donnell was there for her and he understood. They reached the bottom of the steps and Dolly took her hand and led her away.

They stood next to Gemma and Clarissa couldn't believe how Gemma glowed. In just a about a month she'd have another baby.

Lord, please help me count my blessings and put any unpleasant feelings out of my thoughts. She silently asked.

Clarissa stood there and listened to Gemma's plans to make more room in the house for her new baby. Clarissa smiled as she caught sight of Donnell coming her way with a glass of punch. She could really use the distraction. She took the glass he offered and stood next to him so their arms were touching.

"Did I miss anything?" Donnell asked.

"No," Dolly said. "Was there something you wanted to tell us?"

Donnell's brow furrowed. "I can't think of anything. Why do you ask?"

Gemma and Dolly exchanged a look, then they smiled at Clarissa.

"I have nothing to say either."

"Do you think it's possible they don't know?" Gemma asked, amused.

Dolly's eyes twinkled. "I think we should enlighten them."

Clarissa became nervous and reached for Donnell's hand.

"Have you been feeling ill lately, Clarissa?" Dolly asked.

"I've had a few moments but I think it's because of the heat."

Donnell turned to her. "Why didn't you tell me?"

Irritation washed over her. What did it matter to them if she needed to get used to the heat? "I'm fine now as you can see." She wanted nothing more than to go home.

Gemma reached out and hugged Clarissa. "You my dear are glowing brighter than a star in the night sky."

Clarissa pulled back and shook her head. "What's going on?"

Dolly chuckled. "You're going to have a baby."

Clarissa blinked a few times, trying to make sense of what was really going on.

Dolly took her hand and looked into her eyes. "I thought so for the last couple weeks. You my dear are with child. You're pregnant."

Clarissa's mouth opened. She didn't know what to say. She looked up and saw the delight on Donnell's face, and it scared her. "If this is some kind of joke—"

Donnell turned and cupped both her shoulders with his

hands. He stared into her eyes. "How often have you been sick?"

She shrugged and shook her head. "It's just been getting so hot and it makes me queasy." She narrowed her eyes as she looked back at him. "I don't understand."

"I'd pick you up and twirl you around, but I'm afraid it might make you sick. Sweetheart, is it at all possible you are pregnant?"

She couldn't think. She'd been sick almost every day, but that didn't mean… "Oh my! Donnell it is possible. Do you think?"

"He thinks yes," Dolly said excitedly. "I knew it, I just knew it. You have that look about you and I know you've been waiting. Come here and give me a hug."

Clarissa hugged Dolly and then burst into tears.

"That's another thing that happens, you go from happy to sad in a minute flat. I'm so excited for you." Gemma gave her a big hug too.

"Donnell I think I need to go lie down." She gave out a little scream as Donnell swept her up into his arms and carried her home.

"God sure works in mysterious ways. He answered your prayer."

"I have so many blessings it'll take me forever to count them all."

ABOUT THE AUTHOR

Sexy Cowboys and the Women Who Love Them...
Finalist in the 2012 and 2015 RONE Awards.
Top Pick, Five Star Series from the Romance Review.
Kathleen Ball writes contemporary and historical western romance with great emotion and
memorable characters. Her books are award winners and have appeared on best sellers lists including: Amazon's Best Seller's List, All Romance Ebooks, Bookstrand, Desert Breeze Publishing and Secret Cravings Publishing Best Sellers list. She is the recipient of eight Editor's Choice Awards, and The Readers' Choice Award for Ryelee's Cowboy.
Winner of the Lear diamond award Best Historical Novel- Cinders' Bride
There's something about a cowboy

facebook.com/kathleenballwesternromance
twitter.com/kballauthor
instagram.com/author_kathleenball

OTHER BOOKS BY KATHLEEN

Lasso Spring Series
Callie's Heart
Lone Star Joy
Stetson's Storm

Dawson Ranch Series
Texas Haven
Ryelee's Cowboy

Cowboy Season Series
Summer's Desire
Autumn's Hope
Winter's Embrace
Spring's Delight

Mail Order Brides of Texas
Cinder's Bride
Keegan's Bride
Shane's Bride
Tramp's Bride
Poor Boy's Christmas

Oregon Trail Dreamin'
We've Only Just Begun
A Lifetime to Share
A Love Worth Searching For

So Many Roads to Choose

The Settlers

Greg

Juan

Scarlett

Mail Order Brides of Spring Water

Tattered Hearts

Shattered Trust

Glory's Groom

Battered Soul

Romance on the Oregon Trail

Cora's Courage

Luella's Longing

Dawn's Destiny

Terra's Trial

Candle Glow and Mistletoe

The Kabvanagh Brothers

Teagan: Cowboy Strong

Quinn: Cowboy Risk

Brogan: Cowboy Pride

Sullivan: Cowboy Protector

Donnell: Cowboy Scrutiny

Murphy: Cowboy Deceived

Fitzpatrick: Cowboy Reluctant

Angus: Cowboy Bewildered

The Greatest Gift

Love So Deep
Luke's Fate
Whispered Love
Love Before Midnight
I'm Forever Yours
Finn's Fortune
Glory's Groom

Made in the USA
Las Vegas, NV
26 October 2020